30 Guys in
30 Days

30 Guys in 30 Days

MICOL OSTOW

Simon Pulse
New York London Toronto Sydney

SIMON PULSE
An imprint of Simon & Schuster
Children's Publishing Division
1230 Avenue of the Americas
New York, NY 10020
Text copyright © 2005 by Micol Ostow
All rights reserved, including the right of reproduction in whole or in part in any form.
SIMON PULSE and colophon are registered trademarks of Simon & Schuster, Inc.
Designed by Ann Zeak
The text of this book was set in Garamond 3.
Manufactured in the United States of America
First Simon Pulse edition June 2005
10 9 8 7 6 5 4 3 2 1
Library of Congress Control Number 2005921497
ISBN 1-4169-0278-3

For Duy: an unparalleled music editor,
a rising darling of the indie media scene,
and one of the great lurves of my life

Acknowledgments

Many thanks to everyone at S&S: Robin, Bethany, Michelle, and Amanda; to my endlessly supportive family (that's you, Dave!); my friends (who are incredibly understanding of my deadline-related drops from the face of the planet); my fellow Tufts *Daily* drones for a limitless supply of stranger-than-fiction source material; and Jen Love for the original idea of "target practice."

One

8/23, 10:00 p.m.
from: kissandtellen@shemail.net
to: cbclarkson@woodmanuniv.edu
re: first-day jitters

Howdy, little sis—

I just wanted to drop an encouraging line because, if memory serves, you're off to orientation tomorrow, no? How my baby's all grown up . . . (sniff). But I digress.

I'm sure you're stressing at least mildly about heading off to Woodman all by your lonesome. If I can offer you one small piece of comfort, it's that it won't be as bad as you expect. Trust me. I lived through it, and you can too. A few things to keep in mind:

•Under no circumstances should you register for any class that meets earlier than 10 a.m. Even if you think you're a morning person. Even if you have an alarm clock. You will regret it, this I promise you.

•Any activity involving nudity should probably take place indoors. (Don't ask me how I know this.)

•Do not be falsely intimidated by the poetry slam set. Or any set, for that matter. In many ways, college is just a replication of high school, particularly in the perpetuation of cheesy cliques. Don't fall for it!

•Approach all cafeteria food with appropriate levels of wariness.

This may be just about all I have to offer by way of advice, my dear. I understand that Woodman, positioned as it is on the outskirts of the Big Bad Metropolis that is Boston, is slightly different from what I'm used to here at Bryn Mawr. For instance, you'll probably come in contact with some boys every once in a while. But in light of your recent decision to cut the cord with

Mr. Claudia Clarkson, aka one Drew Cordelle, this could be Good News. (Have I mentioned I think you made the right decision? It was time for you to go Cordless for a while. Now all you need to do is declare a major in gender studies and my work will be done.)

If all else fails, remember that I'm always here for you.* Call with anything. You know I love to play the wizened older sister (who is remarkably youthful and exuberant in appearance).

Must run. Daria wants me to start dinner, and the rumor is that I will need to present my senior thesis proposal to the dean of world lit sometime next week. Do ya think a queer reading of the motifs of the female anatomy within third-world feminist literature sounds too dry? Be honest—my academic rep is at stake.

Muchos besos,
Elles

*To clarify, "always" should, in fact, never constitute any hour before 10 a.m. 10 is really a very key hour for me, as I'm sure you're starting to see.

8/23, 11:29 p.m.
from: dcordelle5@columbia.ac.edu
to: cbclarkson@woodmanuniv.edu
re: first impressions

Hi, Bee—

All moved in. Completely exhausted. Wondering if consuming the contents of an entire six-pack of beer on my own was really a good idea.

I arrived at school around lunchtime, and immediately found myself confused. Apparently my dorm had a designated "move-in hour" that I was on the cusp of missing. Fortunately, my RA (shorthand for "resident assistant," as I'm sure you'll soon learn for yourself) directed me to some very energetic freshman males like myself who had come in the day before, unpacked, and were curiously eager to help me unload. I got to pretend that I was a very manly man until we were done—three hours later—and I was outed as weak and unskilled at hard labor. But my new friends were as tired as I! Clearly some relaxation was in order. A quick splash of water across the face and we were "ready to rock" (not my words).

Thus, the beer.

That was three hours ago. An interesting thing about college is that there's no one around telling you what to do. The flip side of that is that there's also no one around telling you what not to do. Like: Don't drink a six-pack of beer all on your own in a span of three hours.

When I realized my motor skills were starting to flag, I made my way back to my dorm, only to discover that my roommate, in my absence, had arrived and unpacked. Buji Kaul. Engineering student. Nice guy, from what I can tell. Rather, uh . . . studious. He was reading a book on quantum mechanics when I came home. We haven't even registered yet, so this must have been a purely recreational endeavor.

Anyway, my tongue is feeling a little less fuzzy, which is probably a good sign. My head, however, is very, very angry at me. I know you're moving in tomorrow, so I wanted to offer some moral support. And, of course, the benefit of my experience, which is to say: The six-pack is not your friend.

College! Crazy, right? I can hardly believe four years have passed since we first met. I know I've said it before, but I am so thankful that you found me and, uh, *encouraged* me to join the newspaper. And then, you know, *encouraged* me to ask you out.

The hangover isn't so great for the nostalgia, I'm discovering.

Anyway, I don't mean to freak you out or question our decision. I think you were right in saying that we needed a chance to be on our owns—back off my grammar; have I mentioned that I'm hungover—for our first time away. Of course, you're the only one who actually went away, really. Columbia's, like, half an hour from Englewood. But that's not the point.

Bee good, Bee (hardy har har) and have an excellent first day. Keep in touch, but don't feel like you *have* to write me back ASAP. I get the independence thing. Of course, if you *feel* like writing, it wouldn't be something that would *bother* me, per se. . . .

Buji just turned off his reading light. I think that's my cue.

Later,
D

Well, this was it. College. For real. It was the last week in August, and I was already deep in the thick of it, actively orienting. Woodman University, undergrad population of 5,367 students, now had one more to add to the mix.

I had arrived at 131 Thompson Hall earlier that afternoon, having braved the Greyhound bus from Englewood, New Jersey, all by my lonesome. (My parents were traveling for business and had shipped my belongings up earlier.)

My first thought upon stepping into my room was that my roommate was a mad Emily Post–Miss America hybrid. It was a tad disconcerting. The bus ride had not been especially kind to me; I was sweaty, scuzzy, and slightly nauseated from one too many roadside Cinnabons.

Charlie, however—that's her name: Charlie, short for Charlotte—was bright-eyed, perky, and fresh. A quick glance around the room told me she had been on a crazed decorating frenzy. The girl had one of those "bed-in-a-bag" deals where the comforter and sheets all match, and they come with about six gazillion throw pillows (why? why?) and something called a "dust ruffle." She had gotten ahold of a color-coordinated "border," which she had already affixed to the upper perimeter of our walls.

Oh, and curtains. And *several* framed prints from the Impressionist period.

It took me about a minute to realize that my own rather simple denim duvet and gray chenille throw were not only going to pale in comparison to her *Trading Spaces* extravaganza, but also clash hideously with same. This could potentially cause problems for myself and my would-be new best friend.

Charlie, however, did not seem at all perturbed by my lack of

1) interior decorating skills

or

2) personal hygiene.

Which was also amusing, given that the girl is a real-life Southern beauty queen. Seriously. Charlie Norton. When I got the roommate assignment over the summer, I Googled her. We had e-mailed casually a few times, which had been enough to satisfy my concerns that we have a tolerable living arrangement.

While I was trying to figure out what

god of computer matchups had determined that a mutual dislike of both smoking and cookie crumbs rendered Charlie "Five-Time Miss Georgia Peach Queen" and myself suitable roommates, she jumped down from her little step stool (something else I'd never have thought to bring along) and stuck out her hand, beaming at me with a level of gorgeosity that rendered me temporarily blind.

"Hey, I've been waiting for y'all! I hope you don't mind that I went ahead with getting the room together! I thought it'd be nice for you to get here and have everything already set up!"

She said this all without a trace of irony. She genuinely seemed to think that window treatments were the key to soothing my fresh-person anxiety.

Her honest-to-goodness niceness, coupled with her "oh, dear lord," blond-haired, blue-eyed, Elle-MacPherson-if-only-she-were-in-better-shape looks, made it pretty hard not to warm to her. As far as first impressions were concerned, I decided that rooming with Miss Manners could have plenty of advantages.

At the very least, there'd certainly never be a shortage of dust ruffles in 131 Thompson. That was something, right?

Orientation seemed to be very much about "getting involved." I was particularly looking forward to getting involved with the ice-cream shop in the campus center, but Charlie insisted that we take more "initiative." (I'll bet she always aced the talent portion of her beauty pageants.) There was an inauspicious-sounding "activities fair" slated for Thursday around lunchtime, and she made me promise to attend with her. I figured there was no harm, and I might even check out the school paper. The thought of seeing my name in type appealed.

I awoke feeling disoriented. I still wasn't used to those borders on the walls. Charlie was at the gym, I knew—shudder—but she would be home soon. I guessed that meant it was time to get my butt out of bed. We'd been up late doing the chatty female bonding thing the night before.

I shoved the covers aside, rose, and walked over to the little dresser-vanity combo that lived behind my bed. The mirror did not pull any punches. Okay, so, it wasn't my finest hour, but there were measures I could take. I ran a brush through my shoulder-length, light brown hair and dabbed on a touch of lip gloss. Better. Maybe not a contender for Miss Georgia Peach, per se, but I could hold my own. I shimmied out of my pj's and into a light blue tank top. Surprisingly, August in Massachusetts was pretty damn humid.

The door opened and Charlie walked in. Seriously, the girl even *sweat* pretty. "Hiya!" she beamed. "Just give me twenty minutes to shower and we can swing by the activities fair."

"No problem," I said. "I'm in no rush. I can even give you thirty, if you want to use the showers upstairs. The ones that aren't coed."

In a nod to egalitarianism, each dorm at Woodman featured one-third coed bathrooms. I was appalled to discover that through some computer glitch, we had landed on a coed floor.

"Oh, sweetie, are y'all afraid of seeing a few harmless boy parts?" Charlie teased.

"Of course not!" I protested—perhaps a shade too vehemently. "Parts are fine. I'm just, uh, not used to stranger parts. I mean, the parts belonging to strangers," I stammered.

"Right, the high school boyfriend," she said, remembering our conversation from the night before. "You guys were together for four years?"

"Yup," I said. "Since freshman year."

"So you haven't been single in ages—and you've never been single on a college campus," she said, rather stating the obvious, if you ask me.

"Well, I mean, neither have you," I said defensively. "Been single at college, I mean."

"Clauds," she said, putting a consolatory arm around my shoulder, "if the look on your face is any indication, then something tells me I'm just a touch more prepared than you are."

She must have sensed that this was a sensitive subject. She gave my shoulder another squeeze. "Don't worry, babe," she promised. "I've got your back."

"Watch your back!" Charlie shrieked, hustling me aside in a mild panic.

I jumped backward in the direction that she was indicating. "What?" I asked, heart racing. We were hovering adjacent to where I *believed* the student activities fair was being held, and I could see no apparent reason for hysteria.

Charlie shrugged and gestured to her left, where a very small, slim, tense-looking boy was carrying a box that definitely weighed at least twice what he did. He dropped it down onto the ground with a thud, sighing heavily and dusting himself off.

"He was going to crash into you. He couldn't see over that box," she said.

"I would have seen her," the boy in question snapped. He must have been wound a little bit tight, because it was pretty inarguable that, left to his own devices, he would definitely have barreled directly into me, possibly causing serious harm. I kept my mouth shut.

"I'm Charlie," Charlie said, offering her hand. The boy shook it, still managing to look slightly peeved.

"I'm John O'Shea," he said. "I'm the editor in chief of the *Chronicle*." He sounded very impressed with himself.

"Oh, right!" I said, hoping to win him over with my upbeat enthusiasm. "We were here to talk to you about that. Don't you guys have a table set up at the activities fair?"

He nodded, sending a thousand face freckles back and forth before my very eyes. It was actually making me dizzy. "We do. But we also have an open-house thing going on at our office." He tilted his head toward the door. "Right now, if you're free." He pointed. "The activities fair is next door."

John walked us one building over, where, as expected, a stretch of tables was arranged in what was actually a rather intimidating amalgamation. Fresh, welcoming faces beamed out at Charlie and me (I swear, the words "fresh meat" must have been branded on our foreheads), calling to us as we passed by: "Do you want to save the children?" "Have you ever thought about becoming a peer-to-peer tutor?" "Stop world hunger!" "Take back the night!"

These all sounded like lofty goals. I was

aiming for something a tad less noble. My byline was beckoning.

"Hey, aren't you into tutoring?" Charlie asked, grabbing my hand and weaving our way over to a particularly well-leafleted tabletop.

"Oh, uh . . . ," I stammered. I thought I had made my intentions clear. But the last thing I wanted to do was alienate my new friend. "I really wanted to check out the newspaper," I said, feeling guilty.

I shouldn't have worried. Charlie couldn't have cared less. "Sure," she said, turning her back to me to beam beatifically at the boy manning the tutoring booth. "I'll just be here when you're done. Or, whatever, I'll come down and get you."

I wasn't wholly convinced of her sincerity, but it did get me off the hook. I figured I should probably wait and see how my own grades panned out before inflicting my study skills on another poor, helpless soul.

I pushed past the activities fair and toward the interior offices of Colby Hall. John had disappeared completely. Once I'd found my way to the *Chronicle,* however, I was disappointed to find that there wasn't a whole lot of open house going on. Walking through the front door I found two tired-looking types standing behind a desk, sorting mail and arguing listlessly. Beyond the front room was a larger, open area, which smelled vaguely of mildew and resembled an homage to a high school news office. Ancient computers sat on rickety desks that scaled the perimeter of the space. Overhead, the walls were adorned with soggy corkboard covered in photos, clippings, and inside jokes that, with any luck, wouldn't be inside to me for too much longer. It was a far cry from the bustling bull pens I'd seen on TV. I turned to a girl sitting at the closest computer. "Have you seen John O'Shea?" I asked. She pointed to the final uncharted territory of the office, a back room where, presumably, production took place. I saw grease pencils, Fun Tack, and oversize tables for laying out pages, and beyond all of that, sitting at some scary über-computer in the corner, I saw John in his multifreckled splendor. I cleared my throat.

"Oh, you came!" John said brightly,

looking up briefly from a monstrous computer screen.

Hadn't we just established this, like, ten seconds ago outside? I wanted to join the newspaper staff. Hence, I came. "Yeah!" I said, trying not to sound confused. Where was the famed "open house"?

"So you, ah, want to write for the paper?"

"Yeah," I agreed. I decided a direct approach was probably best. "Can you tell me a little bit about the process?"

"It's not too complicated," he said, turning away from the computer screen and joining me in the doorway. "Basically, you tell us what you're interested in writing. If we've got something in that department to assign to you, we will—"

At this, the thin girl who'd soundlessly helped me managed a short laugh.

"And, you know, you'll try it out. If we like what you write and you like writing, then you can probably contribute more regularly. After three pieces you go from contributing writer to staff writer, and if you're staff writer for at least a semester, you are eligible to be nominated for department editor."

"Sounds fair," I said, since it did. Also, I wasn't sure why the girl sitting in the main room was practically choking back her laugher.

"That's Megan," John said, clueing in to my complete bafflement. "She's one of the news editors. And she's laughing because, as a daily paper, we will almost always have something to assign to you, if you're game."

"Please. You'd have to be pretty crap not to make staff writer if you wanted," she clarified.

Fab. Thanks for the pep talk.

"Do you have any clips?" Megan asked, suddenly all in my face and brusque.

"Um, do I really need them?" I countered. It didn't sound like they were so selective.

"You don't," John said, glaring at Megan.

Right. Me being the only person at the open house, and all.

"We can assign something to you. Deadlines are five p.m. the day before the article is set to run. You're welcome to come down here and write. Our office opens at ten.

The editors put their departments to bed at nine. When you come down, you'll download your article onto the respective department's disk. Does that make sense?" He looked at me intensely, freckles quivering.

I nodded.

We gazed at each other for an uncomfortably long time. Even John's freckles were still—no small feat, I noted. Finally, I had to break the moment. "Right. So, ah, what should I write on?"

"Yes!" John said, clapping his hands together as if celebrating my incredible brilliance (which he was, of course, welcome to do). "Do you want to cover the Senate's first meeting of the semester?" The look on my face must have given me away, because he quickly amended, "Or, you know, I think there's a 'take back the night' thing. . . ."

"Right, I think my friend's going to that," I said, feeling panicked. I didn't want to reject his every suggestion outright, but then again . . . maybe I did.

John looked at me semi-desperately. "What would you *like* to write?" he asked pleadingly.

I shrugged. Back at my high school I'd been one of the arts editors. But in high school, "arts" meant covering the middle school's rendition of *Fiddler.* I had a feeling it was slightly more competitive here. Still, it was worth asking. "I like, um, plays, and books, and movies, and music," I said slowly.

"Arts!" John said, slapping his hand against his forehead in either relief or despair. "Got it. Cool. Okay, so the person you want to talk to is Gabe Flynn."

He put his hand on my shoulder—surely unnecessary, no?—and rotated me about three feet clockwise. He reached out his hand and pointed. "That's Gabe," he said. "He'll hook you up."

The floor fell out from under me and it was all I could do not to swoon. If you had asked me my own name at that moment, I don't think I could have told you. There was only one thought I could process, and it was quite straightforward:

I for damn sure hope so.

Two

8/27, 9:14 p.m.
from: cbclarkson@woodmanuniv.edu
to: kissandtellen@shemail.net
re: Life-Altering Events

Hey, lady—

Just kill me now.

Since my last e-mail, I have had the questionable benefit of undergoing no fewer than three life-altering events.

"But how?" you ask. Well, college is the time for new experiences, for expanding one's horizons, is it not?

"And so quickly?!"

Yes, I do not fault you your disbelief. And yet. Fate plays no favorites, my dear.

But perhaps I am getting ahead of myself.

"I want to write for the paper," I said, "once I get to college. It's my 'thing,' it's what I *do*. I want to get 'involved.'

"And, by the way, I want to be boyfriend-less."

How do these thoughts tie together? Work with me, sister.

When last I left you, I was a mere naive babe in the woods. Now, Charlie was interested in the orientation "activities fair." She had designs on tutoring her peers and taking back the night, but I myself had eyes for the *Chronicle* and the *Chronicle* only.

Thus, I found the editor in chief, one John O'Shea, who schooled me in the ways of the daily paper. It wasn't complicated. He directed me to one Gabriel Flynn, the chief department editor of the arts section.

Behold: A Life-Altering Event.

You ask if I've spoken to Drew, if I've wanted to speak to Drew, how I feel about the breakup with Drew, and I'll admit, I've had my moments. I've wavered, and I've questioned my decision, to be sure. Oh, but Ellen, if you could have been there, with me, at my side, you would have understood why I solemnly swore instantaneously to waver no more.

Gabe Flynn, you see, is a god among mortals. And I, precious sister, am in love.

Now, I had just selected "arts" out of thin air. I mean, really, I'm not an alterna-girl, I'm no rock diva, and I'm not big into film theory (though, who knows, with my new major in media studies, we shall see . . .).

I mean, there was nothing inherently drawing me to Gabe. Hence, I must fall back on the Fates.

Clearly, it was the Fates that inspired me to "cut the cord" (or any number of puns we've made at poor Drew's expense) that caused John O'Shea to nearly decapitate me (don't ask). And clearly it was the work of the Fates that Gabe *happened* to have two tickets available for Rice and Beans at the Tin Room (that's a group, and a club, respectively. Latin-punk fusion. Keep up, babe).

John pointed me in Gabe's direction. I turned, saw Gabe, and the angels wept (provoked, in part, by a tight T-shirt and thick, styled-yet-somehow-carelessly-mussed hair). I stumbled, momentarily, but regained my composure.

Sort of, I thought, remembering. So I temporarily lost my capacity for speech. These things happen. There are some cultures in which that's considered a certain kind of composure.

It wasn't *that* bad. After a beat, I pulled myself together.

"Hi," I said, so softly that he probably thought he was imagining things. But then he fixed those penetrating blue eyes on me and saw, no doubt, the thin trickle of drool running down my chin. There was to be no further misunderstanding that I was, indeed, talking to him.

"Hi, I'm Gabe," he said, extending a hand.

I shook his hand and tried not to cling to it when it was time to let go.

"I was told you could hook up with me—I mean, that you could hook me up," I stammered.

No matter, I'm told I look better with a little color in my cheeks.

"You wanna write for arts, right?" Gabe asked slowly, looking at me like I had seven heads. Which, I mean, who could fault him, what with the drool and the indecent proposals flying right, left, and center. I wanted to focus on what he was saying, but I was distracted by his voice, which was low and smooth, like honey poured over gravel.

"Yeah, John told me you could assign something to me," I said.

"Okay, well, I've got the latest Mary-Kate and Ashley movie," he said, scooping up a pile of press releases from his desk, "and, um, some open-mic night at the local comedy club."

He paused. I took the opportunity to appreciate his fine bone structure. After a beat, I pulled myself together. "Whatever you've got is fine. I mean, I have to pay my dues, right?"

Gabe shrugged his beautiful shoulders. "Nah, I mean, we need to fill the page."

"Okay," I said, trying to sound agreeable on all points. "What would you recommend?"

Gabe fished a sheet out of the clutter. "Here. This one is a concert. Rice and Beans. Latin-punk fusion. Have you heard of them?"

Um, not so much.

I shook my head. It was safer than yielding to the Tourettes's-like compulsion to open my mouth and confess a secret love of (or, at least, embarrassing familiarity with) Britney Spears. I mean, Latin-punk fusion? What is that? The Pixies meet Enrique Iglesias?

"And the Tin Room is a pretty reliable venue," he continued. "I mean, I almost always like their lineup. There are two passes." He frowned, and sort of squinted at me.

It was a weird kind of look and, to be honest, it made me slightly uncomfortable. This was all fun and games when I was drooling and vibing on my new friend the music-editor-slash-sex-god. But now, suddenly, it felt like he was checking *me* out. And, I mean, I'm not usually *totally* lacking in the self-esteem, but there I was in my Old Navy tank and my Gap jeans, lip gloss a faded memory and hair having seen better days, feeling very unhip and not my most sexy.

For a split second, however, I allowed myself a fleeting hope: Maybe Gabe wasn't about image. Or maybe he'd had enough of the punk-fusion types and was looking for a pop-listening Gap girl. Who knew?

I mean, I couldn't explain it, but there was something supercharged about the moment. Something meaningful in the way his eyes held mine. And for half a second, it seemed like my mad lust-hold was at least partially returned. Was he going to suggest accompanying me to the show?

"*Ugh*, god, not the Tin Room again, Gabe. She's just an innocent freshman. Leave her alone, please."

Behold: Yet another Life-Altering Event.

As I explained, Ellen, I wasn't completely convinced that our Moment was, in fact, mutual. Or even anything more than a figment of my own imagination. But I was willing to step back and see, to let things unfold and marinate in their own due time.

I was in love, you see (again, I'd refer you back to the first Life-Altering Event). My breakup with Drew had a newfound meaning. The Fates had smiled on me.

But the Fates, I was to learn, were a fickle bunch.

I sighed and leaned back in my chair, bathing in the glow of the computer screen. What had happened next was far too humiliating—not to mention demoralizing—to recount.

Was Gabe checking me out at the *Chronicle* office? I'll never know. Because my little love-haze was suddenly broken by a light, airy voice.

A *female* voice.

Said female wafted into the room touching lightly onto the floor with gaminelike legs. The dulcet choir of angels that had erupted into chorus when Gabe first spoke to me? I think they were on loan from this chick. Because now they were pretty much circling her head like a crown of ethereal roses.

"She's just an innocent freshman," the voice said, wrapping one long, lithe arm around Gabe and sidling up to him cozily. "Leave her alone, please."

She smiled at me and extended her free arm. "I'm Kyra. Kyra Hamilton."

I mustered my last ounce of mental and physical energy to return the gesture. "Hi, I'm—"

"This is Claudia Clarkson," Gabe said, cutting me off. "She's our new staff writer."

"I mean, I hope so," I babbled.

Kyra beamed at me beatifically. "That's awesome. I write for features." She flipped a strand of long, wavy hair—so blond, it was almost white—over her slim, pale shoulders.

Features. Cats in trees, I thought fleetingly, imploring myself not to be intimidated by her.

It wasn't working.

"Kyra's the Answer Goddess," Gabe explained, gazing at her adoringly. I couldn't blame him (though I did sort of want to puke). She was the cherubic, towheaded love child of Gwyneth Paltrow and Helena Bonham Carter (with the wardrobe of Drew Barrymore). On my best day, I was the spirit of Christina Ricci (with the wardrobe of a refugee from the J.Crew catalog). If I hadn't hated her for wrenching my one true love from me (and also being my complete and polar foil), I might have adored her myself.

"He's not just being annoying," she insisted. I resisted the urge to make a snarky comment. "I write an advice column, 'Ask the Answer Goddess.'"

"Go ahead, ask her something," Megan

chimed in, actually sounding earnest. "She's like our den mother. Seriously, she gives great advice."

Oh, Answer Goddess, wherefore did thou steal Gabe Flynn's heart? And will I ever love another?

"Oh, hey—all I really need to know is how to get to the Tin Room," I said, keeping my voice as low and steady as possible.

Gabe and Kyra both laughed maniacally as if this were the most hysterical joke anyone had ever told. Which would have been cool, except for the fact that I'd been totally serious. Any hope I'd held that Gabe might want to go to the show with me was completely and utterly dashed. Why had I even been fooling myself? Guys like Gabe didn't want Gap girls.

They wanted girls like Kyra.

8/28, 1:13 a.m.
from: kissandtellen@shemail.net
to: cbclarkson@woodmanuniv.edu
re: Latin-punk *what*?

Heya, sister. Sorry to hear that Gabe is otherwise involved, romantically speaking. I think that buckling down and working on the review is a good plan. After all, that's why you went down to the paper in the first place, right? Focus on yourself, your writing, your classes. You've got your whole first year of college ahead of you. No need to get all hung up on some guy. And I'm not just sayin' that because, well . . . you know . . .

One question, though: Have you ever written a music review? I mean, you know, a review of Latin-punk fusion? I'm just wondering if there's a certain familiarity with the genre that would be helpful. . . .

Never mind. I'm not worried. You'll ace it.

Luv ya, sis. And Daria does too.

8/28, 2:11 a.m.
from: cbclarkson@woodmanuniv.edu
to: kissandtellen@shemail.net
re: Latin-punk fusion

I am *sure* that I will be just fine at reviewing Rice and Beans. I will bring an objectivity to the piece that a more experienced writer might be lacking.

After all, how many critics would be able to compare Rice and Beans with the earlier works of Madonna?

—xx

8/28, 2:27 a.m.
from: cbclarkson@woodmanuniv.edu
to: kissandtellen@shemail.net
re: re: Latin-punk fusion

Maybe I'll just Google the band quickly.
Couldn't hurt.
Right?

RICE AND BEANS LIVE
AT THE TIN ROOM
A Tasty Treat

While the underground punk scene in Boston has, of course, garnered a loyal and lively following since its comeback in the late eighties, one could argue that it's been at least that long since a band brought anything "new" to the genre. Emo, grunge, and even ska are little more than variations on a theme.

We should be grateful, then, for Rice and Beans, a group that dares to blend the strong, frantic bass of post-punk with a smooth samba rhythm. Never

heard of Latin-punk fusion?
Well, good. This is probably the
best introduction you're going
to get.

The five members of Rice and
Beans were at the top of their
game this past Saturday when
they played the blessedly inti-
mate Tin Room. "This is our
first gig outside of New York or
California," lead singer Tim
Hollander announced, before
launching the band into a supercharged rendition of "Eat
This," the first single off of
their cult hit album *Recipes
from the Homeland.* "We're hoping you'll all help us in our
mission to bring Latin-punk
fusion to the mainstream."

Rice and Beans's sound can
only be described as unique, but
they cite their influences as
varied and recognizable. "Yeah,
we're all over the map," bass
drummer Rick Warren told press.
"I mean, The Descendents, The

Sex Pistols . . . and, you know,
Enrique Iglesias. . . ."

8/30, 4:38 p.m.
from: kisssandtellen@yahoo.com
to: cbclarkson@woodmanuniv.edu
re: So?

Don't hold back, babe—how was the show?! Daria is needy to know about the music.

8/30, 5:03 p.m.
from: cbclarkson@woodmanuniv.edu
to: kissandtellen@shemail.net
re: re: So?

Yes, the show. Charlie, god bless her pretty little soul, was more than happy to accompany me (we both felt *mucho* cool heading to a "show" on a random Tuesday night). So after a rigorous day of touring the campus, we cuted ourselves up and off we went.

The bouncer at the Tin Room spent about three seconds examining my press pass and let us in without carding us. The perks of being a bona fide member of the paparazzi.

It was a small venue, dark and dimly lit inside. Crowded, but not thick and oppressive. The floor was beer-stained but thankfully not sticky. In such an environment, I supposed, I could reinvent myself completely, just totally leave behind the whole Gap girl thing. Though, without Gabe around, it was hard to imagine the motivation.

"Oh, my. Did you *see* that guy?" Charlie hissed, grabbing at my arm and sucking all of her breath in at once.

Okay, so maybe *that* was the motivation. There were other fish in the sea, after all.

"Wh—," I began, scanning the room curiously, but Charlie had already begun to shove me in the direction of the back room, where the bar was located.

"We need a drink," she said decisively. And without further ado, she purchased one for each of us.

Apparently what we actually each needed was *three* drinks, which I was to learn over the course of the next hour.

Now, I know we've all seen the after-school special, but there was something to that theory. Something about being drunk that made the music sound a little more sensible to my untrained ear. I mean, I'm not crediting the cheap beer to my stunningly well-rendered music review, but . . . okay, maybe I am. Maybe going out on a Tuesday night to be a cool music critic and hear a cool alternative band really *is* what college is all about. Or so I was starting to think. It sure made sense at the time.

"This is awesome," Charlie shouted, echoing my thoughts and struggling to be heard above the noise (music—I mean music). "I'm so glad you decided not to take back the night." Without warning, the corners of her mouth flipped up, exposing a vast expanse of gleaming white teeth.

For the life of me I couldn't figure out what she was beaming at, so I followed her gaze. Once I'd done that, it was simple to catch her drift: She was blatantly ogling a random if adorable skater guy. And he was ogling her right back. I wouldn't have thought Charlie would go for someone so counterculture, but I guess everyone was looking to expand his or her horizon now that we were officially so . . . *collegiate* and all.

"I think we need another drink," she said to me intently.

"Honestly? I really, really think we don't," I began to protest. At least the "me" part of "we" really didn't. But she had already run off.

I found Charlie—unsurprisingly—at the bar, sucking down a light beer and fluttering her eyelashes at skater-pants, who had somehow beaten me over there. "This is Todd," she said to me. "Todd, this is Claudia, my new best friend."

I was so pleased to hear of my status on the Charlie-o-meter that I didn't notice as she slid a drink of my own across the bar. Instinctively, I reached out and cupped my hand around the pint glass, taking a healthy swig. "Hi, Todd!" I said cheerfully.

Todd nodded at me agreeably. "Hey."

Charlie sipped delicately at her beer. Even sloppy drunk, she was dainty. "Hey Todd, who's your friend?"

I suddenly noticed Todd's sidekick, a

short but muscular guy with a ton of curly brown hair and a T-shirt that said, I HATE EVERYBODY.

"This is Jason," Todd said, shoving Jason forward by way of introduction.

Jason offered a halfhearted smile. He seemed wholly disinterested in me. (But, then again, he hated everybody. It only made sense.)

"How do you guys know each other?" I asked, turning back to much-friendlier Todd. But Todd and Charlie had beaten a hasty retreat, leaving Jason all for me. He didn't look especially pleased about it. Something in my stomach took a dip, but I dismissed the sensation as nerves. After all, it had been ages since I'd been single or out at a place like this. I was out of my element, big-time.

"School," Jason said quickly.

Okay, then.

"Oh, so, um, do you go to school around here?" I asked, taking another stab at making with the nice.

He shrugged. "Not too far."

I was starting to feel about as appealing as leftover Chinese food. You know, how it's always sitting in the back of the fridge and you think you're going to eat it but you never do? That was me. Slimy and cold and all alone in my little white container.

"Um, so do you . . . ," I started, launching a last-ditch effort campaign.

I stopped. Suddenly the thought of cold Chinese food was even less appetizing than usual. In fact, the mere idea of it sent my stomach into acrobatics. A terrible, terrible thought began to form in the back of my mind. And once it had been generated, there was no stopping it from being self-fulfilling.

I was totally going to yak.

Apparently there's something to all of those afterschool specials, after all. Which, really, I wish someone had told me sooner, I must say. Because all I know is that one minute I was standing there talking to Jason-the-Personalityless, and the next minute, visions of kung pao chicken danced in my head. Why, oh why, had Charlie and I ordered from Sun Wah for dinner? It was only a matter of moments before I would be seeing it for real, outside of my head, in reverse.

I clapped a hand over my mouth in a futile effort to prolong the inevitable. Jason, of course, chose this precise moment to demonstrate an appreciable interest in my well-being (possibly because I was turning green). He leaned in questioningly. "Hey, are you—," he began.

But of course he didn't have the chance to finish. Because just as he reached out an arm to steady me, I lost whatever tenuous control I might have had over my gastrointestinal system. With a mighty heave, I bent forward and puked.

All over that stupid I HATE EVERYBODY shirt.

8/30, 5:42 p.m.
from: kissandtellen@shemail.net
to: cbclarkson@woodmanuniv.edu
re: Oooooh

Yikes. I'm not gonna lie, babe—that's pretty atrocious. But on the plus side, it sounds sorta like he had it coming to him? (And at least that gross shirt is ruined . . . we hope. . . .)

So what did Gabe think of the review? Inquiring minds want to know.

8/30, 5:58 p.m.
from: cbclarkson@woodmanuniv.edu
to: kissandtellen@shemail.net
re: re: Oooooh

I don't know yet. I promised him I would bring it by the *Chronicle* by—

Oh, crap.

By six.

Later.

I raced down the hill (much easier than going uphill, I couldn't help but notice), toward what I'd recently learned were the Memorial Steps. I had no idea what they commemorated, but it was a step toward familiarizing myself with campus, at least. At the bottom of the steps lay Colby Hall, the coffeehouse Brew and Gold, and, of course, the *Chronicle.*

I was sweating and badly out of breath, not to mention completely hungover from the night before. No amount of toothbrushing could remove the film of reverse–kung pao chicken from my tongue. Why had I not chosen to e-mail my article to Gabe?

Because I wanted to see him. Right.

Little had I known how closely I would resemble a limp rag when the time came that the deadline approached. A limp, hung over rag.

Rats.

I stood outside of the back entrance to the paper and collected myself, smoothing my hair down and willing my heartbeat to return to its normal pace. Pushing the door open, I saw that I almost needn't have bothered. The office was practically empty—it being a full week before classes actually began, and all. Gabe had told me the paper's deadline was earlier on weekends than during weekdays, and that until classes started, they would be on a weekend schedule. But he had definitely told me to have my article in at six, and it was six-fifteen. Had he already gone home? Now I was nervous that I'd blown it. My first assignment, and I was already behind.

I heard laughter from the main office and made my way inside, relieved. Gabe and Kyra were huddled over the arts computer, presumably reading something on-screen. Love notes? Unlikely. Anna

Bolen, the production and copyediting manager, was leaning in the doorway that led to the production space, glancing over a sheet of paper and seeming extremely bored.

"Oh, hey," I said, feeling awkward. My voice sounded thick and fuzzy to my ears. I cleared my throat and tried again. "Hi."

Gabe turned from the computer and looked up at me. He smiled. "Oh, hey! You're here."

"Am I . . . late?" I asked. "I thought you said six?"

"Yeah, I did," he assured me. "It's really more that *I'm* late. I had to work until five, so I got an extension. Anna here is kind enough to wait around for me." He winked at her. She faked an exaggerated yawn in response, waving her sheet of paper back and forth.

"I totally should have e-mailed this," I said apologetically. "I don't know what I was thinking." I reached into my bag and pulled out the disk with the article.

"Seriously, no worries," he said, taking the disk from me and popping it into the computer. A few strokes of the keyboard, and my document filled the screen. He quickly scanned it. I couldn't bear to watch.

"So, how was your first weekend at, you know, college?" Kyra asked.

"Yeah," Gabe cut in eagerly. "Did you like the Tin Room?"

"It was totally fun," I said, choosing to mentally edit out Operation Regurgitation. "And my friend Charlie was really psyched to have an excuse to go off-campus."

"Yeah, it's hard, because around here, it's really only house parties—which, you know, you have to know someone, or else it's"—Gabe shuddered involuntarily—"frat parties."

"Gabe hates the Greek scene," Kyra said, smiling and ruffling his hair.

Gabe chuckled, leaning in toward the computer again. "Enrique Iglesias!" he exclaimed, reading from my article. He swiveled his desk chair so that he was facing me again. "You did *not* interview the lead singer of Rice and Beans."

I flushed. "Um, not *as such,* no. . . ."

He raised an eyebrow. "So you got that quote from the press release?"

"Well, all I said was that he 'told press,'"

I said defensively. "So, you know, that part's totally true."

"Totally!" he said enthusiastically. "This is awesome. Great job! Have you ever done a music review before?"

I shook my head. "I was on my school paper, but I wasn't a music critic. I was really worried about this," I admitted.

"Well, you came through, kid," he said graciously.

I basked in his praise, but the fact that he had called me "kid" did not escape my attention. He clicked on the mouse, and the computer made a whirring sound. "There. Saved," he said, popping the disk out and returning it to me. "I hope you'll write for us again."

"I definitely want to," I said. I slipped my bag down my shoulder and went to stash the disk. It slid farther down my elbow, though, and when I went to hitch it back up, it flew off my arm entirely. Gabe reached out to grab it before it hit the ground, but only succeeded in overturning it on its way down. The contents of my bag spilled across the floor: disk, wallet, cell phone, lip gloss, dorm keys. . . .

I thanked the god of small favors that it wasn't any particular time of the month, having already reached my weekly mortification quota. I crouched down to gather my belongings.

"Oh, hey, I'm sorry," Gabe said. He stood up out of his chair and kneeled down next to me.

"It's no big—," I protested, straightening myself straight upward and into Gabe's personal space. Our foreheads clunked together with an audible *thud* that reverberated deep within my skull. "Ow," I said, dropping my things again and rubbing my temples.

Gabe seemed to find this all very amusing. "I am such a klutz," he said, laughing. He pulled at my bag and began to reload it purposefully. "Ouch," he said as an afterthought, touching his forehead curiously.

"Don't forget this," Kyra said, reaching out to hand Gabe my wallet. It had somehow rolled over to her feet in all of the commotion. "Oh, and I think this fell out."

Suddenly Drew's earnest face was

beaming up at me. Was I having some sort of concussion? What was he doing here?

"I think this fell out of your wallet," Kyra said again, pushing the photo into my hand.

Of course. My wallet. It was the picture I carried of Drew in my wallet. It had been there so long, I had completely forgotten about it—and, of course, forgotten to take it out when we broke up. It had been a week since I'd seen him—the longest we'd gone since ninth grade. I was completely taken aback. I snatched it out of Kyra's hand and stuffed it back in its place quickly.

"He's cute," Kyra commented. "Very prepster-casual. Who is it?"

"My boyfriend. *Ex*-boyfriend," I hastily amended. What the hell was wrong with me? Seeing Drew's face on a cold-Chinese-food day had set me back a few paces, definitely.

"High school sweetie?" Kyra asked knowingly.

"Yeah. He's in New York," I said. Just thinking about it made me feel nostalgic.

"It's really hard," Kyra said, somehow

hacking into my thoughts. "I've been there. A lot of us have been there. But you will, without a doubt, get over it," she said.

"Don't be sad," Gabe said, chiming in. He put a hand on my shoulder. "You have no idea what this year is going to be like for you." I believed him too. He sounded so sincere.

Kyra abruptly clapped Gabe on the back. "Come on, you. Let's go download her article onto the main drive so that Anna can get to it and go home."

"Oh, right," he said, as if he'd totally forgotten about that. He looked at me carefully, but allowed her to take his hand.

The next thing I knew, Kyra was dragging Gabe into the production office and Anna was giggling maniacally. "Latin-punk fusion," she said, shaking her head. "Ridiculous."

"It *happens* to be a very up-and-coming genre!" Gabe said defensively.

I realized I was the only one left in the editorial office. And I was still sitting by myself on the floor. Slowly I rose and dusted myself off. I slung my bag back over my shoulder and turned to leave the *Chronicle.*

8/30, 10:12 p.m.
from: dcordelle5@columbia.ac.edu
to: cbclarkson@woodmanuniv.edu
re: how ya doin'

Clauds—

That was my *Noo Yawk* impression. How'd it go over?

Not to cramp your newfound college style, but I just wanted to check in and see how your orientation went. I trust you took my word on the whole alcohol thing and kept your imbibing to a minimum. No, I'm serious.

I registered on Friday. The life of an engineering student is not exactly carefree. The prereqs are out of control, and I think the safest thing to do is just to set up a roll-away cot in the library. The good news is that Buji is also in my program. He seems like a good study buddy, although I'm sure we'll either be completely in synch, schedule-wise, or else one of us will have killed and eaten the other by the semester's end. I'm pushing for outcome A, myself. Fingers crossed!

Of course, this e-mail was supposed to be

about you. And so we shall end on that note.
I hope you are well. Be good, Bee.

Later,
D

8/30, 11:27 p.m.
from: cbclarkson@woodmanuniv.edu
to: dcordelle5@columbia.ac.edu
re: fine thanks, and yourself?
Hey, D—
Things are cool—thanks for asking. I tried to
flirt with a guy in a club on Saturday night, but
instead I barfed on him. So, okay, not quite as
seductive as I had hoped, but at least I made
a lasting impression—

[delete]

8/30, 11:28 p.m.
from: cbclarkson@woodmanuniv.edu
to: dcordelle5@columbia.ac.edu
re: fine thanks, and yourself?
Dear Drew—
Thank you for your recent inquiry after my
well-being. As a matter of fact, I may or may

not be in love with my new music editor. Oh! Did I forget to tell you? I'm a cool music critic now. But not the point—

[delete]

8/30, 11:29 p.m.
from: cbclarkson@woodmanuniv.edu
to: dcordelle5@columbia.ac.edu
re: fine thanks, and yourself?
　　Drew-
　　I miss you. Lots. I wonder if we—

[delete]

Three

9/3, 2:54 p.m.
from: cbclarkson@woodmanuniv.edu
to: kissandtellen@shemail.net
re: fun times

Darling Hell-en—

Let's talk about "fun," shall we?

An interesting thing about the word "fun": Two people with otherwise reasonably over-lapping interests can have vastly different ideas about what, exactly, it means.

Case in point: My roommate, one Charlie Norton, a former Miss Georgia Peach Queen and otherwise lovely individual, seems to actively enjoy engaging in the sadistic and torturous ritual known as "the frat party."

For you see, sister of mine, classes begin this Wednesday, and as such, the upperclassmen have begun to return to campus. And with them, so, too, have returned the subspecies known as *classmaticus greekus*—aka: Homo-Fratien.

Now, Charlie's mother was a third-generation Tri-Delt (this has nothing to do with geometry. I already asked), and due to Charlie's dubious "connections," she was invited last night to a bash at Sigma Nu. Determined as she was to drag me out of my little post-puke-age pity party, she recruited me to go with her. To Charlie, the party would be an opportunity to "get my flirt on," as in, to learn to communicate with the opposite sex. Never mind that I'm not totally convinced that I even *have* a "flirt" anymore.

The evening kicked off innocently enough.

"Have I told you how much I *love* that shirt?" Charlie asked. She had, actually. Several times. Not that I didn't appreciate the vote of confidence. It was my favorite shirt: black and stretchy, skimpy but just shy of slutty. Charlie was wearing a sparkly pink halter that tied in about six different places, and of course she looked her typical breathtaking self.

We were standing on the steps of the Sigma Nu house, a redbrick endeavor in the Colonial style so favored by Woodman University. The house was located on fraternity row, or Picard Street, as it was formally known.

"Thanks," I said, glancing down at it and picking off a nearly invisible fleck of lint.

"Don't fuss," she said. "You look great. I love your hair straight. Anyway, I'm sure this'll be fun. They say the trick is to drink heavily."

I opened my mouth to protest, but before I could say anything, a plastic cup sailed out from the window above us, splatting onto the pavement with a wet *smack*, and dousing the bottom of my leg with something liquid (probably beer).

I crouched down to assess the damage. My jeans were soaked.

A thick, beefy head poked its way out of the window. "HEADS UP!" he shouted, then retreated back inside.

Thanks, buddy.

"Oh, no," Charlie said. "Did it get you?"

I extended my right leg by way of demonstration and shook it tentatively back and forth, an impromptu hokeypokey.

"You can't even tell," she proclaimed.

"But . . . what?" Of course you could tell. The entire bottom half of my jeans leg was *soaking wet*. You would have to be . . . well, you would have to be not looking to not be able to tell. Or maybe blind.

"Come on," she said, with finality. "We're going in."

Inside, the house throbbed with energy. The walls pulsed with canned dance music, and the lights were either out completely or were dimmed way down. The house seemed to be illuminated solely by the psychedelic glow of a long chain of Christmas lights.

At least no one would be able to see the stain on my jeans.

"Oh, look, there's Raegan," Charlie said with a squeal. She gestured in the general direction of a tall redhead in the distance. "She wants us to come over!"

I could see no evidence of the fact that Raegan actually did want us to come over

(I could barely see Raegen, for that matter) and, more to the point, I couldn't see any easy way over there. "I'll just wait for you here," I said.

Charlie didn't like this plan one bit. She knit her brows together, thinking. "Okay," she said finally. "You can stay here."

"Mother, may I?" I asked, half-joking.

"Yes," she said, either missing my sarcasm completely or deliberately choosing to ignore it. "On one condition."

"Which is?"

"That you talk to someone. Anyone."

"Huh?" I asked.

"It's simple, Claud. I'm going over there to talk to Raegan. Now, 'over there' is far away and it's kind of crowded, and given that you aren't really interested in rushing—this semester—I'm going to grant you that maybe there's no real reason for you to come with me. But if you're going to stay here, you're going to practice being social."

I stared at her in disbelief. "Do you think I am, um, socially *challenged*?" I asked carefully.

She shook her head emphatically. "*I* don't, sweetie. But *you* do. At least, tonight you do. So maybe you need a little . . . what's that they call it—ah, cognate behavior therapy!" She raised a finger triumphantly.

Her father was a celebrity shrink, I knew. But that didn't mean his training had rubbed off on Charlie.

"You know, when you deliberately behave in a certain way and then, soon enough, your brain follows." She smiled.

"I'm not sure that's the exact scientific definition of the term, Charlie," I replied. The last thing I wanted was to be her social case study.

She shrugged. "There must be *someone* here you're willing to chat with."

I scanned the immediate vicinity. "There," I said, nodding my head toward a perky brunette standing a few feet away. "She's in our dorm. I think her name is Shelley. We were on line together at the yogurt shop the other day."

Charlie wagged a finger at me impatiently. "Dear, y'all are missing the point. You're not gonna talk to some girl from our dorm. You can do that any old day. Tonight, you're going to work on your flirt. Which means that you have to go up to some guy—*any* guy—and strike up a conversation."

That sounded suspiciously easy. "Just walk up to any old guy, and say anything?"

"Uh-huh." She nodded in the affirmative. "Anything you want. It doesn't even matter if he runs screaming in the opposite direction—"

"Thanks, Charlie—"

"Which he *won't*," she continued loudly, cutting me off. "But it doesn't matter, anyway. 'Cause what we're going for here is practice. You need to get out of the Drew zone."

"It's not the worst idea you've ever had," I conceded.

"Awesome!" she said brightly, scampering off.

Alone, I suddenly felt a lot less sure of myself than I had only moments before. *Focus, Claudia. All you have to say is "hi,"* I reminded myself. I took a deep breath and turned to the boy on my left. He held my gaze for a moment. I frantically brainstormed a few openers: *Have you got a light?*; *What's your sign?*; *Do you know where the bathroom is?* and rejected each on its own lack of singular merit (*I don't smoke*; *way too cheesy*; *slightly gross*). By the time I had come up with one, he was gone.

I shoved my way into the common room to find a few stocky boys in *South Park* T-shirts playing a game that involved cups of beer and ping-pong balls. They had obviously been at it for a while, and they seemed like they could be good candidates for my mission. I crossed my arms and leaned against the wall, feeling like a groupie.

After one more round of what looked like people trying to slam ping-pong balls into half-filled cups of beer with paddles (soggy, drunken variation on a carnival game?), a tall, lanky boy with dark hair was proclaimed the winner. "VICTORY SHOT!" he shouted, raising his arms above his head exuberantly and ushering his teammates through the doorway toward what I presumed was the kitchen.

I ran to the bathroom to regroup for a moment. I waited in line briefly. When I was up I locked the door and collapsed against it from the inside. What was wrong with me?

This was a party, for pete's sake, not a job interview. There was no reason to freak out. Okay, so, maybe it had been a while since I'd been in a party-type environment without Drew surgically attached to my arm. Back in high school, we had a system worked out where we separated at parties so that we could mingle with our friends, but we always checked in every half hour or so. Who would I check in with tonight?

Then again, that was a large part of why we had decided to break up. We needed to take some time to figure out who we were.

Apparently, I was a socially inept barf machine with stained jeans.

I stood and splashed some cold water on my face. My hair was behaving and, despite the tropical climate inside of the Sigma Nu house, my makeup was pretty much intact. I wasn't the Elephant Man or a refugee from the "before" part of *Extreme Makeover*. I was a pretty cute girl who, unfortunately, had drank a little too much a few nights before. Duh. Isn't that par for the course for college?

Well, I had managed to give myself a decent mental pep talk when I realized that, for all of my faux-confidence, I was still, you know, hiding in the bathroom. So I popped a Tic Tac and made my way back to the party.

I found the kitchen, which wasn't too difficult (I just followed the sticky beer trail), where Victory and his friends were vigorously attacking a keg. Improvising, I grabbed at a plastic cup and sidled closer to the keg. "Hey," I said, smiling at Victory and holding out my cup. "Can you hook me up?" I had no plans to actually *drink* the beer, of course, but I needed a prop.

"Be glad to," he said, grinning right back at me. He was, at least, pretty cute. He had bright green eyes and thick, sandy brown hair, and even underneath an oversize T-shirt I could see that he was in spectacular shape. I remembered that Sigma Nu was known as "the football frat."

I'd never dated an athlete before—Drew was a total do-gooder/school nerd/student council darling—but reminded myself that the point of this endeavor was just to get the rust out of my system.

All I really had to do was talk to him—which, hey! Mission accomplished. Everything from this point on was just gravy.

Once my cup was full, we headed back to the common room. "You wanna sit?" my new boyfriend asked.

I settled myself on the couch, and Victory sat down next to me. Actually, he was essentially sitting *on* me. I laughed nervously and scooted a few inches back.

"So, you're a freshman?" he asked, leaning into my personal space. I did another small shimmy backward.

"Um, yeah! Well, freshperson." I giggled. How was it that he was back in my lap again? I slid backward. We were playing some weird game of reverse Twister.

"What's your name?" I asked, stalling for time.

He put his hand on my knee. "Kris," he said. He wrapped his free arm around me. We were seriously starting to cross some boundaries here.

"I'm Claudia," I said, holding out my hand to shake.

He looked at my hand, laughed, and pressed it down onto his leg. "Sure," he said, sounding distracted. He leaned his face forward.

Now, Ellen, I may have lost my flirt, but it was plain to see that he was entering the kiss zone, which was *totally* out of the question.

"Oh, look!" I said brightly, pointing off into the distance at an imaginary acquaintance. I jumped up from the couch. "There's my friend Shelley! I'm coming, Shelley," I shouted, waving into thin air.

Kris shrugged and turned to the girl who was sitting on his opposite side, asking to bum a smoke. I guess I'm pretty easy to get over.

I needed to find Charlie and let her know that I was leaving, mission accomplished. I had nothing left to prove and, to be honest, I was tired.

"Easy come, easy go, huh?"

I felt a hand on my shoulder and I spun around quickly. "Huh?"

All of my frustration melted away. It was Gabe. He was the last person I expected to find at a frat party. "I saw the way you handled that guy. Classic."

I ran my fingers through my hair, tense. "I swear, my sex appeal must be totally on the fritz," I grumbled.

"Oh, uh . . ." Gabe frowned and stammered at me. He looked left, then right, then down at the ground, as if he couldn't decide where to settle.

Oh, god, I thought. *Awkward-moment alert. Abort! Abort!*

Color flooded into my cheeks. "Never mind." I exhaled sharply. "God, I am such a dork. That whole scene was a complete cliché."

Gabe burst into nervous laughter. After a moment, he regained his composure. "What are you doing here, anyway?"

"My roommate wants to rush. So one of her sisters—well, would-be sisters—invited her. You know, to check out the scene." I shuddered involuntarily. "It's fun," I said, a shade too enthusiastically, feeling a wave of loyalty to Charlie. "I mean, I didn't have any cool concerts to review tonight, anyway," I said.

"Yeah," Gabe agreed. "You should come down to the paper tomorrow. I've got a bunch of new stuff in. That is, if you want to write again."

"I definitely do. I mean, I will. I mean—" I stopped myself. "What about you, anyway?" I asked. "What are *you* doing here? I thought you hated the Greek scene."

I gave him a quick once-over. He did look vaguely out of place in this setting. His hair was hat-free and carefully mussed (there was definitely some "product" action going on, I decided), and he wore a tight ringer T-shirt that said, VIRGINIA IS FOR LOVERS. His cords were frayed, and his Pumas were two-toned.

He was the anti-Drew, and I loved it.

"'Hate' is a strong word, Claudia," he said, breaking me out of my reverie. He pointed at his shirt. "I'm a lover, not a fighter."

Mmmm, I hope so, I thought. I straightened, trying to banish all inappropriate thought from my mind. "Uh-huh!" I said brightly.

He shrugged. "Anyway, it's Kyra's scene. You know, she was, like, a legacy. So she's Greek. And I'm the moral support."

The words hit me like a punch in the stomach. He was here for Kyra. He was her moral support. He wasn't mine. He wasn't even on the market.

"There she is!" Gabe said, busting into my big, deep thoughts.

He doesn't have to sound so freakin' pleased *about it,* I thought sullenly.

But yes, there she was. She wore a sleeveless printed top that on anyone else would have looked like Grandma's curtains. Her jeans were soft, faded, and stain-free. Her hair was twisted up on top of her head in a style that would have taken me hours to perfect, but for Kyra, I'm sure, was effortless. She probably slept with her hair that way. She was talking to another girl, someone equally casual and good-looking and, from my vantage point, it felt as though I were watching the scene unfold on-screen. It was a movie, and Kyra was the star. But of course, it wasn't *really* a movie. It was my life. Kyra was the star of the movie of my life? When had that happened? It was so unfair.

He grabbed at my wrist. "Come on, let's go say hi. She'll be glad that you're here."

I had no idea why Gabe thought that Kyra and I were destined to be fast friends. The girl was friendly to all, including stray animals, and therefore she'd always be pleasant to me. I mean, I'm sure I wasn't the first chick to crush on her guy, and even if I were, she obviously didn't have any reason to feel threatened. But that didn't mean we needed to be bosom buddies, braid each other's hair, and tell secrets at frat parties. Especially on a night like this, when I was already feeling flattened. No way was I going over there to watch Gabe fawn all over his Answer Goddess.

I was out of there.

Anyhoo, that's my story. But no sense in dwelling. Gabe can't possibly be the last living sex god, can he?

Can he?

—xx

"I can't believe you just went home," Charlie said.

It was the evening after the frat party and we were sitting in the dining hall picking at dinner and rehashing the events of the previous night. Or, rather, I was list-lessly picking away. Charlie was wolfing down her sandwich with gusto. Shelley, who was eating with us, was frowning into her salad. The tomatoes weren't looking very promising.

Charlie swatted at my hand as I reached for another fry.

"Hey!" I protested.

"I'm hungry. There are plenty more fries over at the steam table."

I shook my head. "Not gonna happen." I sunk lower into my seat and zipped up the front of my hoodie. "Tired."

She nodded. "Well, you had a long night," she agreed. "And with a sad ending."

I stabbed my fork toward my salad, chasing a cherry tomato around the bowl. "It was stupid to think South Park could replace Drew."

"Maybe it's too soon to be looking to replace Drew," Charlie offered carefully. "If you're feeling like your sex appeal is on the fritz, maybe you need to get more practice in. South Park might have been a dork-wad, but talking to him did loosen you up. Baby steps."

"So what am I supposed to do, talk to someone new every day?" I grumbled. "File a report with the flirt police?"

"Yes! Well, I mean, not quite," Charlie said, sounding thoughtful. "You don't have to file a report. But you should do that. One guy a day. For thirty days. You know, 'thirty days hath September.' It could be your September thing."

"That's a lot of days," Shelley pointed out.

"And it's September third. We're already behind." I was not liking the sound of this.

"Whatever. It's a good, round number," she said. "Don't get grouchy. You're the one who feels 'rusty,' or whatever you were saying before."

"Does last night count?" I asked. I was intrigued, I have to admit.

Charlie looked thoughtful. "Yes," she decided, after a moment. "Because you were acting on a specific directive when you chatted up Kris."

"Yes, yes I was," I agreed smugly. "One target down, twenty-nine to go." I pulled my hair out of its dirty ponytail and efficiently wrapped it right back up again, trapping any stray hairs that had emerged during my vehement protest of this plan.

"Target?" Charlie asked.

"You know, like, 'target practice.' You pick a target, aim, fire. That's me." I explained.

"I love it," Shelley said, laughing. She furtively crammed a french fry into her mouth.

Okay, so, so far, the most promising guy on campus—Gabe—wasn't a target. Gabe was, hopefully, a friend, an editor, a mentor—albeit an extremely hot one. But he had Kyra. And I had to move on to flirtier pastures.

Me? I may not have had a high tolerance for beer, or Greeks, or even adequately functioning feminine wiles, but I did have one thing going for me:

As of that very moment, I had "target practice."

Four

9/6, 9:58 p.m.
from: cbclarkson@woodmanuniv.edu
to: kissandtellen@shemail.net,
clnorton@woodmanuniv.edu
re: Welcome

. . . to the first official recap of my "target practice." The good news is that I have been able to target, as discussed, one new male a day. The bad news is that I believe my comp sci grade has already been compromised. Curious? Of course you are. Without further ado, then:

(ahem)

The Targets:

• **#1: Kris the Sigma Nu creep.** (Remember,

I met him after midnight, so technically that was Sunday, the first official day of "target practice." Ha-ha.)

•**#2: The random boy** standing behind me at the movies Monday night. I reviewed that new Bond flick for the *Chronicle*, remember? The one I e-mailed you both before it printed? That you promised you'd read and in fact *claim* to have "loved"?

Right, I thought so.

Anyway, I asked him where the restroom was. He pointed. To a huge sign marked LADIES, which was directly to my right.

Embarrassing.

•**#3: Cute soccer-type** perusing the "Local Authors" section at the bookstore on Tuesday.

Me: "Oh, are you taking intro to child psych?"

Target: "Huh?"

Me: (gesturing to the books in his hand) "'Cause of how you've got the intro to child psych book in your hand."

Target: "No, *you've* got the intro to child psych book in your hand. *I've* got the criminology 101 book."

Which, to be honest, he did. It's just I hadn't had such a close look. But really, there's no reason for such hostility. I mean, we're all just trying to get along, right?

Hmmph.

•#4: My new comp sci cutie, whose name is Jesse. Built, blond, caffeinated Jesse. Also known as the reason I may fail this class. I arrived late for class, you see—not particularly auspicious on the first day. I tried to slink as inconspicuously as possible to the back of the room but, in the process of shimmying into my seat, managed to catch poor Jesse's cup of coffee on my festive, if inappropriately wide, "first day of classes" skirt. My professor stopped the entire lecture to bawl me out. I didn't have a mirror handy, but I'm pretty sure my face turned the exact shade of that pink skirt. I whispered a quick apology to Jesse, who, I must say, took the whole thing in stride. Given that he had little dregs of coffee grounds nestled in the ridges of his corduroys.

Welcome to my mortification.

More news later.

—xx

On Thursday morning I popped out of bed earlier than the early bird. Earlier than the worm, even. I was determined to get to my classes on time, and to make a good impression on those professors who weren't already soured against me. I dressed in another "first impressions count" skirt, though I was careful to select one that was slightly more streamlined.

I made my way to the dining hall, grabbing a *Chronicle* on my way inside. I briefly contemplated some scrambled eggs, but the woman behind the counter set me straight with a swift shake of her head *no*. Right, then. I scooped some granola into a bowl, grabbed a plastic container of yogurt and a cup of coffee, and settled into a table off in a far corner, next to a window.

I pulled open the paper to have a look. My review had run in Wednesday's issue, and nothing new had been assigned to me just yet, but I wanted to keep up, both with whatever was going on around campus as well as with whatever was going on at the *Chronicle*.

Blah, blah, SGA meeting, blah, blah, op-ed on the new shuttle system (I fleetingly wondered who in their right mind would have any objection to this service), *blah*

blah, cat stuck in tree, Greeks announce all rush season, new album released . . . bl—

Gabe's music column. I had learned from Anna one evening that an editor could petition for a column by submitting three sample pieces and letting the editorial board vote. That was how Kyra had gotten her advice column—three or four semesters ago—and that was how Gabe had gotten his column, "Heavy Rotation." Columns ran once a week. Gabe's topic for this week was a "back to school"–type theme that drew parallels between the "fresh start-yness" of the fall and the fresh sounds of the indie scenes. I wanted to take notes. All I knew about music I'd learned from listening to local pop stations, and later, from indie-influenced friends at summer camp, but I was woefully undereducated, and suddenly these things mattered to me.

"Suddenly" since I'd met Gabe, of course.

I skimmed down to the end of his column, promising myself I'd check out the bands he mentioned online later. Then I flipped to the back of the paper.

I pulled out a pencil, preparing for the ego-boostingly-easy crossword, when my peripheral vision honed in on something else:

GODDESS: HOT TIMES AT THE LIBRARY, 10 p.m. —ROTATOR

"Goddess?" "Rotator?"
Their column names. *Ick.*
Gabe and Kyra's relationship had penetrated the personals section of the paper.

They weren't the only ones advertising their affections, though. I took a sip of coffee and scanned the rest of the personals. Now that I was slightly more conscious, the little inside jokes practically leaped off of the page at me:

CHIEF: WINGS TONITE. BE IN THE BASEMENT AFTER BEDTIME.

John, we'll order wings after we put the paper to bed.

PRINCESS, IT'S YOUR DAY.

Princess is Megan. It's her birthday—heard her talking about it the other day.

Mind you, there were plenty of personals from innocent, non-*Chronicle*-affiliated students, wishing each other well this semester, saying hello after summers apart. Personals cost three dollars, and it was fun to see one's name embedded within the text. Like silly yearbook messages gone public. One of life's simpler pleasures.

Or so I imagined.

I don't know if I would have reacted in quite the same way if, for instance, John's personal ad had been the first I'd seen. But it hadn't been, so there was no telling. The fact was that this cutesy little game was something that Gabe and Kyra played together. Along with the rest of the *Chronicle.* Not me. Not only was I on the outside of Gabe and Kyra, but despite a couple of well-written (or so Gabe said, anyway) articles, I was outside of the newspaper staff, too.

I felt a lump forming in the back of my throat, a sign of a sudden wave of homesickness. Where had this come from? I'd been at school barely a week. Of course I wasn't in on long-standing traditions or jokes. That would have been way too much to expect, right?

But rationale had no place in my momentary emotional spaz. Memories of Drew flooded back to me: leaving a card in my locker on the first day of school every year, bringing me my favorite chocolate at lunchtime. We had plenty of our own inside jokes and things.

Unfortunately, Drew just wasn't here.

I shoved the paper aside and let my gaze wander out the window. A trio of girls stomped across the quad, arms interlinked. I could only see them from behind, but I was sure, somehow, that they were laughing. And, of course, it wasn't *at* me (seeing as how they were thoroughly unaware of my existence) . . . but it sure wasn't *with* me either.

Pity party, table for one.

"Guess what?"

Charlie soared into our dorm room, executing a quick pirouette and hugging me before collapsing onto her bed.

I looked up from my books. "Share."

I'd been sitting sprawled on my bed, surrounded by reading materials, schedules, calendars, and curricula from my various classes, trying to map out a plan for myself vis-à-vis reading. There seemed to be quite a bit of it expected at school. I was slightly worried.

"I'm going to rush!" she practically sang. Her eyes sparkled, and her mouth flew into a wide grin. "Isn't that fabulous?"

"That's awesome, Charlie," I said. "But I don't get it. I mean, you knew you were rushing, right? This isn't, like, news or anything?"

She laughed. "Well, I wanted to, sure, and I pretty much figured I would, but nothing was definite—until now!" She flopped backward so that she was lying down and facing the ceiling.

I recalled the article I'd seen in the paper that morning. "Oh, yeah. They had sign-ups or whatever?"

"Registration," Charlie corrected me dreamily.

"So you're going to go Tri-Delt, like your mother—right?" I asked.

Charlie sat up suddenly. "Oh, Claudia,

I keep telling myself to keep an open mind, that I might be more interested in another sorority than the Tri-Delts, but I just know, deep down, that that's not true. I *do* want to be Tri-Delt, just like my mother." Her eyes were wide with sincerity.

"I'm sure you will be," I said, meaning it. In addition to having bazillion generations of legacy, Charlie was basically a dream sister. I mean, the girl was born for this type of stuff. In a good way.

She gnawed at a fingernail nervously, then stopped once she realized what she was doing. "I don't know, Claud. It ties my stomach into knots just thinking about it." She suddenly sat up. "Come with me?"

"Uh, no," I said shortly.

"Why not?" she pleaded. "It would really make me less nervous. And it would be so much fun! Something we could do together as roomies."

I glared at her. "We go to the dining hall together. 'As roomies.' Isn't that punishment enough?"

"Seriously, Claudia—I need you. The sisters, the parties, the judging . . ."

"And you think *I'll* be able to help you

deal with that?" I asked incredulously.

"*Definitely,* Claudia. Y'all have a very calming effect on me. Remember that time we were in the bookstore and I couldn't find the book I needed, and then you knew where it was."

"Charlie, that wasn't me being 'calming,' that was me clueing in to the alphabetized shelving systems," I insisted.

Charlie shook her head, undaunted. "I don't care, the point is, I was all worked up, and you were so practical about it, just checking the shelves. That's why I need you."

"To read shelves," I repeated dubiously.

"To be my wingman!" she enthused. "Wing *woman*!" She took an excited breath. "Whatever! It'll be *fun*!"

"Oh, I don't know, Charlie," I hedged. "Sometimes we have different ideas about fun."

"Well, that's true," she conceded. But she wasn't a quitter, that Charlie Norton. "What if," she said, leaning her forearms against her knees and adopting a solemn expression, "we make a deal?"

"What kind of deal?" I asked, skeptical.

"Well, you'll register, and we'll go to some events. And if you hate it, you can drop out. No questions asked."

I scowled at her. "One party. That's it."

She flung her arms around me and squeezed for dear life. I coughed.

But who was I to have such a negative attitude about all of this? I mean, eight hours ago I'd been lamenting my lack of "niche," my sense of not belonging? And here was someone literally begging me to join in—to join her, and to eventually, hopefully, become a part of something larger. I didn't really have a good reason to turn her down, short of a very hazy and probably biased idea of what it meant to be Greek.

I was, of course, having doubts. Charlie, meanwhile, was having her very own MTV party to go. She was doing her Beyonce impression down the narrow space between our beds. I had to laugh. Charlie was fun. Hence, rushing with Charlie would probably be fun.

Probably.

I stood and joined her in a grand finale. Then I straightened up and smoothed my skirt out.

"Where are you going?" Charlie asked as I scooped my wallet and keys into my bag.

"I have to pick something up in Cambridge," I explained. "At the Coop." The Coop was the Virgin Megastore of college bookstores, located smack in the center of Harvard Square. Anything you couldn't find at the Woodman bookstore, I was told, was sure to be available there. I was banking on locating some software for my computer science class. We were supposed to bring it to our next tutorial, and the thought of showing up empty-handed gave me goose bumps. The bad kind. Our professor, Hartridge, didn't seem easy-going at all. "Do you need anything?" I asked.

"Nuh-uh," she said, winding down from her sudden burst of activity. "Well, maybe some sour peaches from that candy store. Are you taking the shuttle?"

"Yup."

"It leaves from the campus center," she pointed out smoothly.

"Yes, Charlie." I sighed. "I'll sign up for rush on my way."

9/8, 11:01 p.m.
from: cbclarkson@woodmanuniv.edu
to: kissandtellen@shemail.net,
clnorton@woodmanuniv.edu
re: I'll admit it . . .

I had a moment (or two) of hesitation as I signed my name—and my upcoming Friday night—to the rush sheet. I put the pencil down, then picked it up again, suffused with an urge to cross out my name. But I reminded myself that I was doing this strictly as a favor (got that, Charlie?), and that I could stop the instant it became un-fun. Of course, that assumed there would be a time when it was *not* un-fun. Or, rather, that it was fun. My doubts were actually starting to become sort of confusing.

I was mulling over this rather complicated thought process as I walked down the stairs of the campus center to the first floor, where, if my sources were correct, the safety shuttle would arrive momentarily.

"Ow!"

"Oh, god," I said, stepping back. While descending the last step, I had somehow managed to stomp directly onto an innocent passerby. "I'm so sorry—I'm such a spaz. I was just—well, I guess my mind was wandering."

"Hey, no harm done. Though I may send you a bill for the concussion."

I laughed. "I'm Claudia. Clarkson. And I'm *really* sorry," I said again.

"I'm Dave," my victim said. "And it's fine."

I reached out to shake his hand, and finally got a look at him. Dave was tallish, and thin without being heroin-chic gaunt, with floppy, light brown hair. He was smiling and had a friendly, open look about him, further underscored by the fact that he was choosing not to press charges over our little hit-and-run.

"So, what were you so incredibly wrapped up in, Claudia Clarkson, that you nearly killed me?"

I flushed. "I'm a little bit embarrassed. My roommate has me rushing with her. You're not Greek, are you?" I asked suspiciously.

He shook his head. "Nope, not me. But some people think it's fun. Right, Gabe?"

Come again, friendly Dave? *Gabe?*

Sure enough, loping toward us was Gabe, whistling to himself and bouncing a little bit as he walked. It was pretty cute, I had to admit, even if I was taken aback.

Apparently so was Gabe. "Wh—," he began, then stopped when he saw me.

"Gabe, this is Claudia Clarkson," Dave said, introducing us. "She's my friend who just caused me bodily harm."

"It was an *accident*," I insisted, giggling, "but actually—"

"We know each other from the paper," Gabe finished. He looked a little bit nonplussed.

"Yup, he's my muse," I said. Maybe having Gabe's cute friend around had somehow detracted from the Gabe-related speech impediment that usually set in right about now?

"Some of Gabe's best friends are Greek," Dave said affably. "I pass no judgments. But, hey—you work at the paper, so you must know Kyra!"

"The Answer Goddess." I tried to suppress the sarcastic edge that swelled inside of me.

I mean, correct me if I'm wrong, but I *think* I was just starting to find the flirt zone, was I not? And here they were, to plague me again: the media supercouple of the Woodman campus. They were like Woodman's own Jennifer and Brad. Or, I mean, Jennifer and Ben. The *other* Jennifer and Ben. Or whatever. Why can't these Hollywood couples just make it work, anyway?

"So, where are you off to?" Gabe asked.

"I have to run some errands in Cambridge," I explained.

"Oh, you need to check out that CD shop right next door to the Coop!" Dave said, suddenly animated again.

"No way, man," Gabe said, intensely. "That place is beat. Totally overpriced." He looked at me. "There's one in Porter that's better. The next time you're down at the paper I'll give you the address."

Dave shoved his friend lightly. "Whatever, Claudia, do yourself a favor. I mean, if you're going to be at Harvard *anyway,* you might as well check out the place by the Coop. Even though Angsty Musician Man doesn't condone it at the moment."

I had to laugh. "We'll see if I have time, guys."

But the scene was starting to feel a little bit stale, and I couldn't put my finger on why. Maybe it was their respective—freakish—determination that I shop where they shop. It was weirdly competitive, almost.

I needed some fresh air. And, anyway, the shuttle was on its way. Which was what I told them. I thanked them, and then I made my way to the shuttle.

Things I learned about boys in general today:

•They are very serious about where they shop for CDs.

•They can be very open-minded about the Greek system under the right influences (i.e., cute girls).

•They can be gracious in the face of bodily harm.

•It *is* possible to have a normal conversation with one!

Things I learned about Gabe, in particular, today:

•He is VERY serious about where he shops for CDs.

• He will go to frat parties only when accompanied by Kyra.

• He is oddly territorial of his friends. Which is a shame, because under different circumstances, I sure wouldn't mind running into Dave again. But whether or not Gabe's taken, I don't want things to be weird between us. And there are definitely at least two thousand male undergrads I still have yet to meet. So why sweat the small stuff?

—xx

9/8, 11:59 p.m.
from: kissandtellen@shemail.net
to: cbclarkson@woodmanuniv.edu
re: Dear, sweet—

—*naive* Claudia: Is it possible that Gabe was merely jealous? After all, it does sort of sound like you were vibing on his friend. A lot of guys—even guys with girfriends—get bent out of shape about stuff like that.

Or so I hear.

"What do you think?" Charlie asked, twirling so as to give me a more accurate full-body view of her gorgeosity (which, I will admit, is impressive). In preparation for our rush "cocktails," Charlie wore a slip dress in a sleek gunmetal gray shade, and strappy shoes that looked dangerously uncomfortable. She had set her hair in hot rollers so that blond waves now tumbled over her otherwise bare shoulders, and her makeup managed to pick up on the subtle shimmer of the dress without making her look like a runaway Christmas tree ornament. I was impressed. She had clearly picked up some skills in the Georgia Peach beauty pageants of the past.

As an act of supreme kindness, she had even extended her expertise to me in a consultory role. I wore a lacy black skirt that just skimmed my knees, and a soft pink cashmere tank top that Charlie assured me complemented my light brown hair and brown eyes. Me, I was just going for as much comfort as I could, right down to the simple ballet flats I wore on my feet. "Very Hepburn," Charlie had appraised, making a thumbs-up gesture. "Audrey, I mean."

"Thanks," I replied, taking a moment to touch up my eye makeup.

"Claudia, I really wanted to tell you again how much it means to me that you're doing this," Charlie said.

I felt a tinge of guilt. "Charlie, I told you, I'm just giving it a try. I promised I would go to this event tonight and keep an open mind—I certainly don't think there's anything wrong with rushing, or pledging, or whatever. *But,* I really do want to get more involved at the paper, and if I don't want to stick with the rushing, you have to be cool about that."

"Of course!" she insisted, giving me an enthusiastic but mindful-of-our-swanky-clothing squeeze. "I promise you I will. No worries, no hard feelings."

She sounded sincere, I had to admit. But I was worried, nonetheless. It was the look in her eyes.

Two hours and twenty minutes later, which was two hours into "cocktails," and the look in Charlie's eyes had intensified to one of utter awe. I had to admit that the Tri-Delts were classy. Or, at least, their sorority house was. Again, it was a Colonial style house built of red brick, but it was nearly twice the size of the Sigma-Nu house and vastly cleaner, which just goes to show about the fairer sex. Cocktails and mingling were being held in the sitting room, which, as near as I could tell, was a fancy word for a living room, just off of the enormous dining area. Charlie sat on a chaise in the far cor-ner, sipping a Cosmopolitan and telling an elaborate anecdote that somehow involved quite a bit of enthusiastic, tinkling laughter and the tossing of her hair back over her shoulder. This party was the flagship event of the rush period, intended to kick off the week as a "getting to know you" among all of the sisters of the various houses and all of the potential rushees. But, somehow, Charlie had practically become the primary attraction of the evening. I felt an odd and perhaps misplaced sense of pride. I also felt a sense of relief. If I decided that I didn't want to do this, the girl would clearly be okay without me.

"Do you need another drink?" I looked up to find a very petite, very perky girl with short blond hair holding a silver serving tray laden with flutes of champagne. Another sister. I shook my head and tilted my own Cosmopolitan at her by way of demonstration.

"Oh, great," she squeaked. She set her tray down and plopped onto the overstuffed chintz chair next to me. "We were worried that no one was drinking the Cosmos." She pointed at her name tag. "I'm Meredith. I'm Chi-Omega."

"Hi, I'm Claudia," I said, exposing my clavicle so that she could see my own tag.

"Are you excited about rushing?" Meredith asked. She must have been able to read my guilty expression, because she quickly lowered her voice, "It's okay. That's the whole point of coming to these things. To see if it feels right. Please. Some of my best friends are my sisters, but my closest friend at Woodman was my freshman year roommate!"

I smiled. "It's actually my roommate who wants to pledge." I cast my gaze across the room to where Charlie was leading her loyal followers in an impromptu Macarena.

Meredith glanced over to the small pop video in progress. "She should have no trouble at all," she offered. "But what about you? What do you like to do?"

I took a sip of my Cosmo, then set it back down again. "I like to write," I offered. "I did two reviews for the *Chronicle*. I'm a little bit high on my byline."

Meredith smiled. "I'm sure," she agreed. "I love the *Chronicle*. Everyone on campus reads it. If you write for that regularly, you'll be a minor celebrity."

I liked the sound of that. "I can live with that," I told her.

"Oh! You should write a column!" she continued. "My friends and I loooove to read the columns. Our favorite is . . . what's it called?"

I had a sinking feeling. "Um, 'Ask the Answer Goddess'?"

"Yeah! We love that one! The Answer Goddess rules! What's her name?"

"Kyra Hamilton," I said tightly, trying not to scream. Was it impossible to go twenty-four hours without hearing *someone* extol her virtues? She was out of town this weekend, I knew, so I had thought the rush event would be safe. But it turned out that no place on campus was safe. Dammit.

"Yeah, exactly!" Meredith said triumphantly, as though I had just read her the secret formula for turning lead into gold. She sighed wistfully.

So did I.

9/10, 1:14 a.m.
from: cbclarkson@woodmanuniv.edu
to: kissandtellen@shemail.net
re: first things first

That is to say, I don't think I'm going to rush. Although all of the young women I met tonight (well, technically last night, but since I still haven't gone to bed yet . . .) were friendly, outgoing, and actually surprisingly un-Stepfordian, I have a feeling that comp sci, the paper, and any other form of life I choose to have this semester will actually take up enough time that I don't need to do this. Something tells me Charlie will rush hard enough for the both of us. Elles, she was *totally* the belle of the ball last night.

Okay, full-disclosure time.

But as I tell you this I want you to please KEEP IN MIND that I was definitely not going to rush, regardless. I had already made my mind up about that before . . .

Before . . .

Okay, I'm just going to have to come right out and tell you.

It was the Cosmos. That or the cool "smoky eye" makeup that Charlie had helped me with. And my weird conversation with Gabe, where he was acting like a spaz. And that flirtation with Dave. For some reason I had gotten it in my head that I was a reasonably attractive girl who would, in fact, someday discover the secret of communicating with the opposite sex. Clearly I was deluded, punch-drunk on my assault-and-misdemeanor of the previous afternoon. But there I was, chattering away with Meredith (who is *way* too interested in the *Chronicle* for her own good, if you ask me), when I started feeling pretty good about myself. I mean, the sweater was really comfortable, and my hair was up and out of my face. My long-wearing lip gloss was wearing on and on . . . I didn't necessarily want to rush, but here I was, making friends, having conversations right and left. Sure, I was no Charlie Norton, supported as she was by throngs of admirers, but I absolutely felt like I belonged. And it was just that very false sense of security that completely did me in.

Because two hours into the party and three hours into rush cocktails, the boys arrived.

The party was in full swing. Suddenly the doors were open to the remainder of the campus and, specifically, members of the opposite sex. Meanwhile, I was buzzed, I was cute, and I was in a damn good mood.

Watching the boys pile into the house, I vowed to myself that I would seize on the opportunity to re-enact the Dave scenario (minus internal bruising) with the first hottie I saw. You know, walk over, strike up a conversation, maybe make a joke or two . . . and, sure enough, ten seconds later and not a moment too soon, he materialized. Tall. Blond. Hotness a cool 9.8 on the kiss-a-bility scale.

Bingo. Target #6.

I thought about bumping into him accidentally/on purpose, since the bumping thing had worked so well with Dave. Or spilling coffee on him, as I had with Jesse. But those incidents had been unplanned; and as premeditated efforts, both of those techniques struck me as desperate and awkward, the moves of a rank amateur. And I was past that stage, wasn't I?

Wasn't I?

I decided I was. In which case, the idea of asking him for the time, or which way to the bathroom, seemed equally immature and unappealing. No, I was going to have to go for the gold. And, judging from the fact that he was fast turning to make his way to the kitchen, I was going to have to do it quickly.

I sidled on up to him as surreptitiously as I could, given that he was six feet three to my cool five feet four. "Hey," I said, beaming at him for all I was worth. I tried to toss my hair like Charlie, before remembering that my hair was up in a ponytail. "Hey," I repeated, slightly running out of steam. I took a deep breath and forged ahead. "I'm Claudia."

Cutie of the evening smiled at me. "Hi, Claudia," he said. "I'm Zach."

I wracked my brain for something clever to say, but my brain, dulled by one too many Cosmopolitans, did not want to help me out. "Aren't you in my comp sci 5 class?" I asked, knowing he wasn't. Okay, not my finest work, but a solid effort, nonetheless.

He bought it, though. He shook his head, grinning. "Actually, Claudia, I'm an engineer. So I placed out of those requirements."

So, no remedial math for you. Check.

"But, uh, hey—I could tutor you, if you want. If you're, you know, having a hard time."

Well, hello there, Mr. Tutor-man.

I was feeling pretty proud of myself for a minute there. All I really needed was a cute cashmere tank and a little Cosmo-induced come-hither chutzpah and suddenly I was a flirt machine. Wasn't an offer to tutor practically as good as a date?

I decided it was. "Yeah, I would totally love that. Hartridge *hates* me," I purred. *Purred!* I was purring! It was the fuzzy knit wool against my skin, I was sure.

"Nah, he's just grouchy," Zach insisted. "Besides, if we can get your grades up, it really doesn't matter what he thinks of you, right?"

"Sure, whatever," I cooed, lowering my eyelids in what I hoped were bedroom eyes.

"So what else are you taking this semester, Claudia?" Zach asked, leaning in close to me and lowering his voice.

"Mass media and the popular culture," I said.

"Cool. Watching television for credit."

"Exactly," I said.

"I can help you with that homework too," he offered. "My television is just down the street."

Oh.

"CLAUDIA!"

I spun to see Charlie standing up from her chaise lounge, hands rooted firmly on hips in a superhero's pose. A supremely pissed-off superhero.

I flashed another blinding smile at my new hottie and hurried over to Charlie. Once I was within three feet of her, she grabbed at my wrist and pulled me aside, fuming. "Are you *insane?*" she stage-whispered.

"No," I said hotly, "Are *you?*"

"Claudia, that is Zach Masters. He's president of the Inter-Greek Council!" she said, still with the fake-lowered voice.

"Um, okay, then. Still not seeing the reason for the hissy fit."

Charlie smirked at me. I realized it was the first time since I'd met her that she had smirked. I was actually sort of relieved to find that she was willing and able to smirk, come to think of it. "No," she said. "But he goes out with Anu Shah, the president of the Panhellenic Sisterhood!"

"Oh!" I said, matching her stage whisper with one of my own. Then, as it sank in, *"Oh."*

"Right," she said, the anger in her voice giving way to weariness. "And she is standing over there"—she pointed subtly to the dining room—"and she *completely* saw you macking on her boyfriend."

I sighed. "Oh, Charlie, I'm sorry."

"Don't be sorry to me," she said. "He's not my boyfriend. And, anyway, he's the one to blame here. It makes me really mad. But you should know. I mean, you can't go out with him."

"Of course not!" I said, horrified.

"And, um, based on the look she's giving you, I'm not so sure about your chances at Tri-Delt."

I laughed. "Charlie, I don't think I'm going to rush," I said, glad to have it out in the open.

"What? No, you can't bail out! Not because some skanky chick's boyfriend busted a move on you! It's not your fault! And if she really does try to keep you out of Tri-Delta, we'll totally report her. I made a lot of connections here tonight," she assured me.

"I don't doubt that," I agreed. "But this isn't my scene, and besides, you don't need me for this, right?"

She nodded slowly. "I guess not," she said reluctantly.

I vowed to Charlie that we would have plenty of other opportunities to do things together as roommates, and that I was rooting for her all the way. I also tried to stick around for a little while and not feel too uncomfortable just because good old Anu was giving me the fish-eye. But it didn't work.

Elle, I'm lost here. I mean, either I'm barfing on boys in bars, or choking out lame questions that no one responds to (except, of course, to feel sorry for me), or, when I finally do manage to meet and sustain conversation with someone reasonably attractive and intelligent, he's either the best friend of my spontaneously socially awkward editor, or he's the boyfriend of the woman with the power to make my roommate's life miserable.

Anyway, I gathered my jacket and bowed out of the party as gracefully as possible, avoiding Anu and Zach at all costs. They must do this little dancey thing pretty often, because when I left I noticed them making out in the corner.

So, you know, more power to them. Ain't love grand?

I wouldn't know.

—xx

Five

9/10, 6:13 p.m.
from: cbclarkson@woodmanuniv.edu
to: kissandtellen@shemail.net,
clnorton@woodmanuniv.edu
re: me, circa noon today

Waiting outside of Dunkin Donuts (What is it with Dunkin' Donuts, anyway? It's, like, some sort of zoning law that there needs to be one every three blocks or so. Is it a Boston thing? Why? Why?) for the student shuttle to take me from the center of town back to campus. Semicute prepster waiting on line for said shuttle as well. Khaki carpenter cords, rumpled plaid flannel shirt, all-terrain sneakers.

So not my type.

But that should make it easier, right? I mean, if there's nothing, really, at stake. Objectively speaking, he's attractive, in a crunchy, trust-fund kind of way. Says I to myself, *Self, I think I'll just mosey on over and say hi. Target #7, I presume. . . .*

Is that weird? (Other than the moseying, that is. The moseying is *definitely* weird.)

But just walking up and saying hi, I mean. Do people do that? People other than strange, hormonally challenged college students stranded in Boston with no sex appeal and no recourse to speak of, that is?

I was losing focus, and fast. So, going up and just saying "Hey" was clearly out of the question. But what else was there?

Can't ask him for help with my bag, I thought. *It's, like, some Q-tips and a bottle of hairspray—nothing I can't lift. Can't ask for a light, because—what if he gives me one? I don't smoke; that's definitely weird. . . .* "What time is it?" *Yeah, except I'm wearing an oversize G-Shock in electric blue—highly inconspicuous. Not.*

All right, I got it. Walk. Walk, dammit!

"So, is this where we wait for the shuttle?" *Smile at him. With teeth.*

Fewer teeth, Claud.

He's looking at me. He looks surprised. He's nodding.

Ah, yes. He's pointing . . .

. . . to the huge yellow sign directly overhead, marked, WOODMAN UNIVERSITY SHUTTLE PICKUP.

I see.

"Thanks!"

Yeesh.

Thank you very much, ladies and gentlemen. I'll be here all week.

—xx

By Sunday morning I decided I had to study, lest my many trips to the bookstores of Cambridge—not to mention so many rides on the safety shuttle—be wasted. My handy-dandy reading schedule suggested that today would be an ideal time to address chapters one through three of a particularly dense and nonillustrated text on the spread of AIDS in North America. I took one look at the book and tossed my pop culture anthology into my messenger bag instead. I threw on some track pants and a long-sleeve T-shirt, my favorite broken-in sneakers, and a denim jacket and made my way across the residential quad and down the hill to the library.

In the two weeks since I'd arrived at Woodman, summer had truly begun to give way to fall, and the air outside was crisp and cool. The sun sparkled off of the surface of the buildings on Picard Street, and the color of the grass seemed bright and rich. Despite Friday night's flirting debacle, despite the fact that Professor Hartridge hadn't really appreciated my little coffee incident, and despite the fact that I was *definitely* on the verge of running out of clean underwear and had *no idea* where the laundry room was, things were looking up.

The library was quiet, which of course, wasn't unusual, it being a library and all. I bypassed the computer lab with its dangerously tempting high-speed Internet access, and traveled straight through the Great Hall, a tremendous room with stained-glass windows known for being a hotbed of social activity. I finally settled on a cozy cubicle in the far corner of the reading room. I tossed my bag down, pulled my iPod and my books out and, within moments, was deeply immersed in the issue of Complicity and Viewership: The Active and the Passive Audience Examined.

I read for about an hour or so. All was well in the world of studying when, out of nowhere, Eminem went from whispering in my ear to screaming straight into my brain. Highly soothing. Not. "What the—," I began, confused and more than a little bit annoyed. I grabbed my iPod and quickly turned down the volume.

That's when I heard it. Chuckling. More specifically, *Gabe*-style chuckling coming from just behind me.

I whirled around and glared at him. "Very funny."

He was laughing so hard, he was practically crying. "I'm sorry, Claudia, I couldn't resist. You just looked so focused."

"That's the whole point," I fumed. "The focus." But it was really only fake-fuming, at this point. Gabe was wearing a long-sleeve T-shirt with the Atari logo emblazoned across the chest. How could I stay mad at that?

"What were you listening to?" he asked, swiping my iPod from me before I had the chance to protest. He scrolled through my playlists. "Eminem—not bad."

"Please. Just because I don't wear faux-vintage-eighties apparel doesn't make me any less hip than you," I said, wondering furtively where I could get a T-shirt like Gabe's.

Was this banter? Were we having banter?

"Touché," Gabe said, pulling up a chair next to mine and settling in. "And, anyway, I got this shirt in a thrift shop in the suburbs, so I should probably mind my own business." He eyed my Pumas. "Cool kicks."

"As it happens, I got these sneakers in the city," I said, smirking at him.

"New York City?"

"Yeah, I'm from Northern Jersey," I explained. "My friends and I would go shopping downtown on weekends."

"Cool," he said, saying the word slowly so it came out almost like an exhalation: *cooool.* . . . "We don't really have anything like that back in Highland Park."

"Where's that?" I asked.

"Illinois. No great shakes. Just your run-of-the-mill suburban town. Like something out of a John Hughes film."

"You are *not* knocking John Hughes films," I admonished him.

He held up his right hand in the peace sign. "Save Ferris," he deadpanned. But before I could swoon, he turned his attention back to my iPod, a thick chunk of hair falling over one eye. I longed to reach out and brush it back for him, but decided that would be overkill. After all, this was really our very first maybe-banter. I didn't want to push it. "You've got some cool stuff on here," he proclaimed.

"Yeah?"

"Yeah, The Get Up Kids are, like, my favorite. Although, Claud—"

"Yes?" I cringed.

"The Backstreet Boys have got to go."

"Um, I think my younger cousin stuck that on there. What do you recommend in exchange?"

He paused for a moment, looking thoughtful. "Well, I've got a lot of stuff you should sample. But I bet you'd really dig Death Cab for Cutie and the Postal Service. The Shins. Interpol. I could burn it all for you."

I couldn't have been more psyched if he

had offered to marry me. Or, okay, maybe that's not strictly true, but still. "That'd be awesome."

"Yeah, when you come down to the paper, I'll give you a disk."

I frowned. "We haven't exactly discussed when that would be. I keep scanning the personals to see if maybe there's some cute little hidden message waiting for me, but so far, *Rotator,* no dice."

What? Where had that come from? Mild-mannered Claudia Clarkson had unwittingly been overtaken by a snark machine.

Gabe, however, seemed either oblivious or impervious to my sarcasm. "Yeah, the personals. It's just this lame-ass thing we all do. I can't even remember who started it. It probably began way before my time. But, you know, we're all down there for so many hours, it gets late, and we've had too much sugar. The next thing you know—"

"Cheesy inside jokes printed for all the world to see," I finished for him.

"Yup."

"I can relate. You'd be shocked at the things I do when I'm on an M&M's rush."

"Really now?" Gabe said.

I was suddenly aware that Gabe was in the kiss zone. I mean, not kissing me, not even planning on kissing me, clearly, but still. There he was. In my face—in a good way. I *could* kiss him . . . theoretically. This was an extraordinary head trip. After all, I was having banter with a taken man. Someone else's boyfriend. I could tell myself he was flirting, but deep down I knew ours was the banter of platonic friends.

"Oh, yeah." I wound the cord from my headphones around the machine and tucked it away into my bag. I checked my watch. While I didn't particularly want this exchange to end, if I didn't hurry, I was going to be late meeting Charlie. I'd promised to run through her Spanish vocabulary with her.

"Can you meet me at Brew and Gold on Wednesday afternoon?" Gabe asked. "I can stop by the *Chronicle* office and pick up a new assignment for you."

"Hmmm . . ." I spent a few seconds staring off into the distance and pretending to be much busier than I actually was. I mean, who was I kidding? The boy could have offered to meet me in the seventh circle of hell and I would have been there with my sunglasses on. "Yeah, that should work. I have pop culture until six, though."

"No problem. Come by around seven. That gives me time to get down to the office and sort out what we've got for you."

9/11, 9:58 p.m.
from: cbclarkson@woodmanuniv.edu
to: kissandtellen@shemail.net
re: Monday was . . .

. . . a blur. My comp sci professor, Professor Hartridge, caught me asking my seatmate/target, Brett, to borrow some scrap paper, and went into severe conniption mode. He demanded that I work through some programs on the board. In front of the entire class. Brett, of course, could offer little more than a sympathetic grin. I staggered through the exercise with the panic of a caged rabbit, trying to block out Hartridge's barbed comments as I doggedly puzzled out the latest program.

He is *definitely* still irked about that coffee sitch.

Child psych on Tuesday was no better. I wasn't completely sure that my professor actually spoke English. Or, if she did, I was kind of worried, because she wasn't using any words I recognized. Then again, I was tired. Poor Charlie has one more week to go of rush period and has taken to stumbling into bed at odd hours of the night covered in strange substances like whipped cream, chocolate sauce, and jam. (Is she making some sort of elaborate human sundae?)

So I wasn't exactly in top form, though I did manage to offer a reasonably lucid argument in favor of the passive viewer in my pop culture class that my professor seemed to support. Or, at least, she didn't verbally abuse me, which, after Hartridge, was really the most I felt I could ask for.

So there I was, fastening my messenger bag and slinging it over my shoulder, when it occurred to me that it was already six o'clock and I didn't yet have a target of the day taken care of. I glanced around. Everyone else was similarly gathering their belongings and getting the hell out of Dodge. This wasn't good. I needed a Target #9, and I needed one bad. . . .

There! In the blue rugby shirt. Or, actually, the shirt was purple—okay, a little bit strange, but beggars really can't be choosers, now, can they? I snaked my way through the obstacle course that was our seating area, willing purple shirt to maintain a steady pace. Just as he was about to cross through the doorway, I reached out and grabbed firmly onto his big, purple polo collar.

He made a choking noise and staggered to a halt.

I scampered around so I was facing him and smiled demurely, going for casual. "Hey!"

"What gives?" he asked, sounding sullen. Also, sounding a little bit hoarse, for which I blame myself.

"Hey, um, we have a paper due in a few weeks in this class, right?" I asked.

He glared at me. "It's on the board, moron." He stalked off.

Ah, yes. The board.

And so it was.

What I left out of my e-mail was what happened after.

I heard applause and laughter from the direction of the teacher's desk.

Laughter that I was definitely starting to recognize.

"Claudia, are you *always* trying to beat up on strange guys?"

I shrugged. "Only the cute ones, Gabe. And what are you doing in this class, anyway?"

"It's add/drop period until Friday, Claud," he said. "We can audit whatever classes we want and petition to join. I just got added to this class."

I swallowed. If this was true, it meant that I'd need to start paying closer attention to personal grooming on Tuesdays and Thursdays. I didn't know if I was ready for that. "But you weren't here during class."

"No, true. I only arrived in time to see your fists of fury in action."

"Please. It was far less aggressive than you make it sound," I retorted, huffy. "I only wanted to ask him a question."

"Uh-huh," Gabe said knowingly, jerking a thumb at the blackboard casually.

"Whatever," I said. "You're the one who's, like, my *stalker.*"

"You wish, Claudia," he said, reaching out and pinching one of my cheeks between his thumb and forefinger.

Of course, he was right. And so I didn't really have an answer for that.

"So you're telling me he just, like, suddenly showed up in your class?"

"Uh-huh. So, you—*huh*—think it's—*huh*—weird too—*huh*?"

"*What?*"

I gathered my breath together. "So you—*huh*—think it's weird too?"

Charlie leveled me with a look. "Claud, I think you're going to have to kick the three-packs-a-day habit. Really. I'm worried about you."

"Ha—*huh*—ha." It was all I could cough out.

Charlie had managed, against all my better judgment and years, *years,* of sedentary living, to drag me to the school gym. She had been a hard-core runner in high school and was already beginning to go through withdrawal. "Not to mention," she'd explained to me grimly the night before, "I'm not sure I'm going to be able to get away with the late-night pizza parties if I give up the running completely."

"Okay, fine, but that's *you,*" I'd argued.

"Why should I be made to pay the price for your active, healthy lifestyle?"

Needless to say, it was not a compelling argument, and nine a.m. Wednesday saw me sweating away on the elliptical machine, clutching at the arm holds for dear life. "You know—*huh*—Charlie, it occurs to me that I never really did—*huh*—consult my medical professional before—*huh*—undergoing a new exercise regimen." I blew a stray wisp of hair out of my face and resumed my desperate, sucking inhalations.

"Can we go back to talking about cute boys?" Charlie asked, knowing full well that it was the only way to stop my complaining. Whatever. The girl needed no distraction. For that matter, she didn't even really need me there. Thirty minutes we'd been slogging away like hamsters on a wheel, and not a single strand of Charlie's hair was out of place, her breath was even and measured, and she was having no problem whatsoever carrying on a simple conversation. It was seriously annoying. Even her sweat was pretty and pert, trickling down her temples like she was shooting a commercial for a sports drink.

"Yes, *anyway*," I continued, "I just— *huh*—thought it was weird that he just, you know, *showed up* in my—*huh*—pop culture class."

"Well, I mean, it *is* add/drop, Claudia. A lot of people are trying out different classes at the last minute. And, besides, did he even know that you were *in* that class?"

"*Huh!* Okay, not exactly," I admitted. "I'm not saying he's, like, secretly in love with me. Just that it was a pleasant surprise to see him show up unexpectedly like that. And who knows? Maybe we can be study buddies or something."

Charlie snorted. As surprised as I was that someone like Charlie would do something as indelicate as snorting, I was amazed that she had enough aerobic control to actively snort. "Please. If Kyra lets him."

"She's not the boss of him," I protested.

"No, she's just the girlfriend of him," Charlie pointed out—rather meanly, I felt.

"*HUH!* True enough," I said sadly. My machine admonished me to PEDAL FASTER. *Forget that,* I decided.

"I'm done," I said with finality. I dismounted and wiped myself down.

"Why?" she asked, looking genuinely surprised that someone would ever cut a workout short.

"Because when an inanimate object starts issuing me directives, I need to draw the line while I still have some small measure of control over my own destiny."

"Come back," she pleaded. "I'm sorry about Gabe. I just don't want you to have unrealistic expectations."

"Believe me, I don't," I said shortly. "No need to worry."

"When are you seeing him again?"

"Tomorrow. At the paper. Or rather, on top of the paper, at Brew and Gold. He's got another assignment for me."

"Oooh! Another gig at the Tin Room?"

"I should think not," I said, narrowing my eyes at her. "You remember what happened last time."

She giggled. "Not really."

I shuddered. "Exactly," I said, and began to wander off.

"Hey, wait!" she called from her perch. "Where are you going?"

"I want to do some weight training," I explained.

She wrinkled her forehead in surprise. *"Really?"*

I laughed and jerked my head in the direction of a stocky, athletic type bench-pressing over by the Cybex machines. *"'Target practice,' baby,"* I clarified, and sauntered on over.

9/13, 2:43 p.m.
from: cbclarkson@woodmanuniv.edu
to: kissandtellen@shemail.net
re: I'd like to preface . . .

. . . this e-mail by saying that this "target practice" thing really hasn't, for the most part, been nearly as painful as I would have expected. Sure, there have been a few bumps and glitches here and there: choking that guy in my pop culture class, sure, not a high point in my college career. Or, you know, that loser, Zach, who turned out not only to be taken, but to be taken by someone who was at the party where I met him? Yeah, awkward.

So sure, there were some embarrassing moments. But that was just, you know, part of the fun. And then. Just when I let my guard down, when I think that, maybe, just maybe, I'm learning to relate to the opposite sex, I somehow find a way to humiliate myself in some novel and spectacular fashion.

As, for example, at the gym.

I can just hear you now, Ellen—"What were you even *doing* at the gym to begin with? Nothing good can come of that!"

I know. That's always been my motto, after all. All I can say is that it was a favor for a friend. And that favor has been paid in full.

Well, said friend (CHARLIE) was thrashing away next to me on the elliptical machine like Jennifer Garner on crack, when I noticed him. Target #10. Clearly an athlete. Thick, muscular, well-built . . . like a tank. He was prone, flat on his back on a weight bench. Different barbells and dumbells of varying heft lay to his right and left. He reached for one, grunting.

Enter Claudia Beth Clarkson, stage right.

"Hey, need a spot?" I asked brightly.

(A "spot" is when you stand very close to the weights in case the person who is lifting them needs a boost or is having trouble or something. See? I know these things.)

Anyway, so there we are, Tad—his name was Tad, I learned—having finished his last "set," and standing. And he's kind of looking at me, checking me out, and suddenly I'm realizing that I'm really only wearing some tight black yoga pants and a stretchy blue tank top. Which, suddenly, just does not feel like all that much.

"Hey," Tad says, "I've got an idea."

Note to self: For future reference, avoid gym-related "ideas."

"Why don't you let *me* spot *you* for a while?"

In fact, Tad was *already* doing plenty of spotting, but I could hardly say no, seeing as how I'd been all chatty. "Um, sure. But, ah, which machine?" I asked nervously. Keeping in mind my fundamental dislike of physical activity, of course.

He gestured to a scary torture device standing against the far wall. "Squats," he said. It sounded like a death sentence.

The would-be iron maiden was, in fact, a legitimate training device. Tad led me to it and showed me how to position myself. He tested the overhead bar and asked me how much weight I could hold.

"I can probably hold my own," I

bragged, suddenly overcome with a need to impress this random person I'd known for all of five minutes. It was insanity, I tell you. And it was to be my ruination.

"Oh, yeah?" he said casually. He looked me up and down once again, and I was once again grateful for the extra layer my sports bra provided. "I'll bet you can. Your legs look pretty strong." He eagerly loaded what felt like blocks of cement to either side of the bar.

"Go for it, babe," he called, stepping back. "Twelve reps."

I smiled and gathered my strength. I leaned down to release the bar. *"UF!"*

Yeah, that bar? It was pretty heavy.

Once I'd gotten the bar free from its starting point, things happened quickly. The barbell bore down on me at roughly the speed of light, and I nearly sacrificed my kneecaps in a desperate attempt to stay upright. All the air rushed from my chest and I began to make, I'm sorry to say, some not-very-feminine sounds. It's entirely possible—I'd even go so far as to say likely—that my face turned beet red, sweaty-shiny, and that I spit. But of course I wasn't looking in a mirror or anything, so this is all pure speculation.

To his credit, it only took Tad about three seconds to realize that something was drastically wrong. Unfortunately, they were the longest three seconds of my life.

They were also the three seconds during which, I am sorry to say, the left leg of my yoga pants and the right leg of my yoga pants decided to part company.

Oh, that's right. They split right down the middle.

Now, it's possible that I would have been able to conceal this fact with a witty little "Oh, Tad, you're such a card, I'm just going to, ah, back away into the corner to spontaneously take off my tank top and tuck it into the back of my pants because I'm so amazingly, incredibly hot. . . ."

Or some such.

But that scenario would have required my remaining, if not upright, at least in some way grounded for the duration of the experience. And, sadly, that was not the case.

Tad rushed over (to his credit—and to my extreme surprise—paying no mind to the gaping hole in the crotch of my pants) and, true to his designation as "spotter," lifted that barbell straight off of me, placing it back in its starting position (using only his pinkie finger, of course).

Myself? Well, I was thrown for a loop by this sudden shift in equilibrium, my sense of balance thrown completely off. Did I go down?

Sure. Going down wasn't so much the issue.

It was going down and *over* that really brought it all home.

It was like something out of Cirque du Soleil. That is, if Cirque du Soleil featured dancers wearing crotchless tights (which, when you think about it, really would make it an entirely different kind of show). Tad stared at me for a beat or two, taking in the horror of the scene. Then, all at once, he shuddered, as if waking from a nightmare. He was then kind enough to toss me his discarded hooded sweatshirt to tie around my waist, and to offer me a big, meaty paw to help me to my feet.

I was endlessly thankful for the shirt. But, of course, the damage was done. Half the gym saw me (and there's no way they could have missed my show, what with the glorious Technicolor and surround sound, to boot) and my sad, laundry-day panties. Even Tad, trying like hell to pretend he wasn't mortified on my behalf, looked, well . . . mortified on my behalf. Completely.

But he did let me wear his sweatshirt home.

—xx

9/13, 3:12 p.m.
from: kissandtellen@shemail.net
to: cbclarkson@woodmanuniv.edu
re: Oh, dear
Wow, Claud, that's really . . . um . . .
I mean, I'm sure no one . . .
You shouldn't be . . .
Okay, just *how* badly did the pants rip?

9/13, 3:17 p.m.
from: cbclarkson@woodmanuniv.edu
to: kissandtellen@shemail.net
re: re: Oh, dear
I hate you.

On Wednesday afternoon, I ran some errands in the hour I had between class and meeting Gabe, then slowly made my way over to the Brew and Gold. It was buzzing this time of day, after most classes had ended but before most students were ready to start thinking about dinner, studying, or other evening plans. Students were curled comfortably in the overstuffed sofas and chairs provided, hunched over reading or holding quiet conversations with their neighbors. It felt to me exactly like a college campus was *supposed* to feel, with lots of young people talking, thinking . . . *being*. For the second time that week I found myself happy, again, to be at Woodman. I went up to the counter and ordered what had become my regular: a double espresso with a shot of vanilla. I paid for my drink and made my way over to the side bar. Once I'd poured an entire cow and three packs of sugar into my drink, I backed away.

Which was when I saw Gabe.

He was on his way in, and he looked tousled and tired. His hair stood up in strange patterns, and his T-shirt (Scooby-

Doo) was rumpled. There was an unidentifiable yellow stain on his cords. And he was wearing glasses. Thick, black, Buddy Holly glasses over his beautiful hazel eyes.

I couldn't help myself. I loved him yet. "Gabe!" I called out, waving to him. He looked up, brightening when he recognized me.

We wandered toward each other and met in the middle of the coffeehouse, sinking down in an unexpectedly vacant love seat. Gabe unshouldered his bag and collapsed against the back of the sofa. "I am so wiped," he said, sighing heavily. "Pop quiz and then a review that needed to print, like, yesterday."

"Oh, I didn't see it," I said. Normally I made it a point to always read his reviews.

"I know you didn't," he said, winking at me. "You didn't even read the paper today, did you?"

I blushed. "Well, not yet," I admitted. "I—"

"Hey, did you change your hair?" he asked suddenly, cutting me off. He sat bolt upright in his chair and reached forward to touch it.

I froze in place. "Um, I just blew it out straight today," I explained. "Sometimes I do that."

"I never noticed before," he said, looking puzzled.

I was pretty darn puzzled myself. Since when did Gabe Flynn take note of my hair? Kyra must have schooled him in such things.

Thinking about Gabe noticing Kyra's hair made me depressed. "Why—I mean, how did you know I hadn't read the paper?" I demanded, covering.

Gabe grinned. He reached down into his bag and pulled out the day's *Chronicle*. He quickly paged through to the back and slammed the paper down on the coffee table in front of me. "There," he said, pointing his index finger to the personals section:

CB—ARTSY—FANCY AN ANI-FEST?

I glanced at him. "ARTSY? Me?"

He nodded enthusiastically, clearly proud of himself.

I felt strange and tingly inside. All the

blood rushed to my head. I couldn't believe that Gabe had played the little personals game with me.

I couldn't believe I hadn't read the paper that day!

"Cute," I said, trying not to squeak with excitement. "But how would I have known that was meant for me?"

"Well, my dear, if you'd been *reading* the paper for which you've been *writing,* then you would have just sussed it out, intrinsically. You start to get a feel for these things when you've been with us long enough."

"You make it sound like a scary cult," I protested. "And what's an 'ani-fest,' anyway?"

"You know, like an animation-fest. Spike and Mike's Sick and Twisted; Wallace and Gromit; etc., etc. . . . every year Boston holds its own roundup of the best new animated shorts on the scene. Most of the major distributors are there to scout. It's really fun. Would you be into it?"

"Yeah, definitely," I said. "I love animation. I was a huge fan of *Family Guy.*"

"Me too! I have a T-shirt," Gabe said.

"Here," he said, rummaging back in his bag and coming back up with a crumpled press release and some passes. "It's Saturday. This will admit you plus one guest." He paused. "Man, I'd love to go."

For the second time in twelve seconds, I froze. I would have been happy to invite Gabe along, of course, but it would have just been inviting pain upon myself. I mean, Saturday night was date night. If Gabe wasn't going to the animation fest with Kyra, it was because they had other plans. But, then . . . why did it feel like he was hinting to me?

Because you wish that he were.

"*There* you are!"

I looked up.

Gabe looked up.

Kyra beamed back down at us. She wore a long, gauzy skirt skimming her ankles and grazing the floor, a sleeveless top accentuating her dancer's frame. Her hair was wound up on top of her head and she looked, as usual, radiant and ethereal.

She sidled on up to Gabe and immediately began to run her fingers through his hair, reconstructing it as I had longed to do when he first walked into the coffeehouse. "Everyone's looking for you downstairs," she said. "They need you to once-over an article before they can put it to bed."

Gabe stood, smoothing out the front of his pants in vain, and straightening his glasses. "Sure thing," he said.

"Um, so, about the animation fest—" I started hesitantly.

He thrust the press release at me. "Here you go. You should call beforehand to let them know you're coming, and who your guest will be."

"You're going to cover that? Perfect," Kyra cooed. "Gabe asked me, but I really can't stand cartoons. It's too hard to take them seriously."

"Um, right," I agreed, for lack of anything better to say.

Kyra linked arms with Gabe. "Come on, babe," she said, turning on her heel and dragging him with her.

Each put one foot in front of the other, and they were off.

I sat, alone with my scrunched-up pieces of paper, my personals ad, and my nondate with Gabe. I felt like the least desirable female this side of the I-95. I turned to the target—umm, *boy* sitting one couch over. "Do you like animation?" I muttered halfheartedly.

He glanced up at me briefly, then looked back at his book. "Nope."

Great, then.

9/13, 5:45 p.m.
from: cbclarkson@woodmanuniv.edu
to: kissandtellen@shemail.net,
clnorton@woodmanuniv.edu
re: 11 down, 19 to go . . .

Yeah, I'm going to an animation-fest. Alone.

—xx

Six

9/15, 9:42 a.m.
from: cbclarkson@woodmanuniv.edu
to: kissandtellen@shemail.net,
clnorton@woodmanuniv.edu
re: coed naked hijinks

So, just popped into the coed bathroom for a shower and, um . . . accidentally walked in on one of my coed neighbors in his birthday suit. Fun times. I've never seen a human being jump quite so high into the air, save for sporting events and the like.

Does that count as Target #12? Survey says: sho' 'nuf.

"So, uh, what are you taking this semester?"

"Huh?"

I snapped out of my reverie to find my dinner companion, Cameron, snagging yet another fry off of my plate.

For the record: I sincerely dislike it when people take from my plate without asking.

Of course, that was but one of the various ways in which Cameron had managed to irk me, big-time, since he and Troy had arrived to pick me and Charlie up for our ill-fated double date.

I blamed myself, of course. Charlie had met Troy at the gym. Something to do with their eyes meeting across a valley of treadmills. Anyway, he'd asked her out and she'd said yes before hearing the catch. The "catch" being Cameron, his best friend in from Amherst for the weekend. Charlie had begged me to come along, and I had foolishly agreed.

It started when they arrived fully twenty minutes late with nary a phone call, text message, or smoke signal to indicate that they were running behind schedule. Lack of punctuality: another huge pet peeve of mine. Then there was the fact that when they did arrive, the very first thing Cameron did upon our introduction was unabashedly look me up and down, his gaze sweeping across my body like some kind of high-security surveillance camera, only to then step back, slide his tongue out of his mouth ever-so-slightly, and murmur, "Dude . . ." with a wry thumbs-up in Troy's direction.

I mean, gross.

I tried to explain my position to Charlie on the car ride over to the restaurant. "This is a problem," I whispered fervently. "I do *not* blow out my hair for boys who use the word 'dude' as an adjective!" She shot me a dirty look that I took to mean that she wouldn't have me ruining her night with Troy, and leaned forward, asking Troy to "crank up the tunes."

Dude.

Of course, I was soon to learn that I needn't have been flattered or even surprised by Cameron's behavior. The minute we walked into the restaurant, he immediately cast his oh-so-discerning eye over the female members of the waitstaff. I fled to the ladies' room for a brief respite. There was only so much "dude" I could take in one night, after all.

Fast-forward to the dinner, where Charlie was sitting across the table practically in Troy's lap, having basically left me for dead, while I picked listlessly at a burger and tried my best to appear at least marginally interested in Cameron's prattle. Which was harder than you might think.

"I asked what you were taking this semester," he repeated, sounding slightly annoyed.

Okay, so maybe I wasn't *exactly* trying my best.

"Um, I'm taking . . ." Suddenly I couldn't for the life of me remember my own schedule. Was it possible that in talking with Cameron my IQ had actually shot down ten points? Was he *that* toxic?

Without warning, his hand slid up my leg. *Question answered.*

"Do I make you nervous?" he taunted.

He had little bits of french fry sticking to the corners of his mouth.

Nervous, no. Nauseated, yes.

I scuttled over to my own corner of the booth. "I'm taking computer science, and intro to pop culture, and, uh, child development, biology, and women's history," I rattled off.

"Oh, women's history," he said knowingly. "No wonder you're such a priss."

"Um, excuse me?" I said, quite certain that I'd misheard him.

"Feminist," he said shortly, stuffing more of my dinner into his fat mouth.

I stared at him in disbelief. "Yes, that's exactly it," I deadpanned. I glanced over at Charlie, who, at this point, was officially making out with Troy at the table. That, or performing emergency mouth-to-mouth. *Is this behavior really becoming of a Georgia Peach?* I wondered.

I thought about storming out in a huff. That would have at least made for a good anecdote. But Charlie would have definitely caused me serious bodily harm. Not to mention, we were at least ten miles from the nearest T station and I really didn't have enough money on me for a cab. I was in it for the long haul.

"Are you, uh, finished with that?" Cameron asked, pointing a beefy index finger at my hamburger.

I sighed and pushed my plate toward him. It was going to be a mighty long night.

9/17, 1:19 a.m.
from: cbclarkson@woodmanuniv.edu
to: kissandtellen@shemail.net,
clnorton@woodmanuniv.edu
re: blind dates

Valid "target practice," yay or nay?

I'm saying yes. And then I'm going to bed. And never agreeing to another fix-up as long as I live.

—xx

9/18, 11:01 a.m.
from: cbclarkson@woodmanuniv.edu
to: kissandtellen@shemail.net,
clnorton@woodmanuniv.edu
re: deep thoughts

From the animation-fest, according to Mike Nugent, design major at Emerson: That if you play Season 1, Episode 12, of *The Simpsons* backward and on extended-time release, it will reveal the identity of JFK's killer.

Whatever.

Target #14, all accounted for. At least I'm almost halfway there.

Am running out of things to say re: the

festival. Have little further opinion other than, of course, abject fear. I mean, some of those men were wearing *costumes.* Tights: Not a good look for the forty-plus and balding set.

—xx

9/18, 5:17 p.m.
from: cbclarkson@woodmanuniv.edu
to: arts@chronicle.woodmanuniv.edu
re: ani-fest
<Attachment>
   Here's the article. Sorry I'm late. Let me know if you have any problems opening it.

9/18, 6:03 p.m.
from: arts@chronicle@woodmanuniv.edu
to: cbclarkson@woodmanuniv.edu
re: re: ani-fest
   Claud—
   Looks great. Sounds like you had an . . . interesting time? ;)
   Check the personals tomorrow.

   —G

9/19, 1:53 a.m.
from: cbclarkson@woodmanuniv.edu
to: kissandtellen@shemail.net,
clnorton@woodmanuniv.edu
re: grrr

My right brain is mad at my left brain. Or possibly the other way around. Which is it that controls logic and which controls creativity? Does it even matter?

I'm fried.

I have a comp sci quiz in approximately eight hours that I was made aware of, um, about eight hours ago. Good times.

Oh, and Target #15? Pedro, the handsome and virile delivery boy from Mexicali Rose.

I think we'd have fine-looking children.

—xx

9/19, 2:04 a.m.
from: clnorton@woodmanuniv.edu
to: kissandtellen@shemail.net,
cbclarkson@woodmanuniv.edu
re: Um, no.

I'm sorry, Claud, but I have to put my foot down. Delivery boys *do not* count as "target practice."

9/19, 2:21 a.m.
from: kissandtellen@shemail.net
to: cbclarkson@woodmanuniv.edu,
clnorton@woodmanuniv.edu
re: Come now

Oh, Charlie, can't you see she's suffering?

9/19, 3:37 a.m.
from: dcordelle5@columbia.ac.edu
to: cbclarckson@woodmanuniv.edu
re: Surprise!

Hi, babe!

An interesting thing I learned last week: Surprises come in many shapes and forms. Like the surprise quiz I was given in my English class. That was a good time.

Then there's the surprise of the culinary variety. As in, the "tuna surprise" that our dining hall just loves. I really can't get enough of that.

And finally, my true favorite: the surprise visit. Generally practiced by close friends and romantic partners. Such as Buji's long-distance girlfriend. I know what you're thinking—who knew Buji had a long-distance girlfriend? Not me—which makes this a *double-layer* surprise!

Now Bee, we're living in close conditions here, and I'm really not wanting to cramp my man Buji's style. So I thought I'd take the opportunity to come up and visit. Surprise!

Just friendly, hon. I promise. But I do miss you.

Let me know what you think.

Later,
D

9/19, 6:16 p.m.
from: cbclarkson@woodmanuniv.edi
to: kissandtellen@shemail.net
re: fw: Surprise!

Crap crappity crap. Just failed a comp sci quiz. Definitely, completely failed. My average is totally sunk.

Oh, and one other thing. Yeah, got an e-mail from Drew last night. Scroll down. Read it and weep.

And then let me know what the hell you think I should do.

—xx

9/19, 6:43 p.m.
from: kissandtellen@shemail.net
to: cbclarkson@woodmanuniv.edu
re: Oh my

Well, what are your choices? You can either tell him, politely but firmly, that you don't want to see him; or you can offer to host him. I guess the question is what you would rather do. I mean, if you tell him no, there's a good chance he's going to be offended. You have to be okay with that. And if you do want him to come, and you don't want things to go to the boyfriend-girlfriend place, then you're going to have to be strong enough to keep things on the friend level.

Tough choices, dear. But they are *your* choices to make. Don't forget that.

9/19, 7:01 p.m.
from: cbclarkson@woodmanuniv.edu
to: dcordelle5@columbia.ac.edu
re: Surprise!

Hey there—

You know I'm a sucker for a surprise (unless it's of the tuna variety. I hate that stuff. Blech). I assume you'll be in on Friday? The bus from

Port Authority will take you straight to Boston's South Station. I can meet you there. It's really easy. E-mail me with the particulars when you've got them.

:)

—xx

CHRONICLERS CAN ROLL WITH THE PARTY DOWNTOWN MIDNIGHT.

9/20, 11:43 a.m.
from: cbclarkson@woodmanuniv.edu
to: kissandtellen@shemail.net,
clnorton@woodmanuniv.edu
re: Targets and weirdness

Picture it, if you will: The room was bathed in glittering, psychedelic hues, and classic disco was being remixed to neo-trance beats by a crazed, Afroed DJ set in a booth ten feet above the rink. I was on my second beer and having kind of a hard time matching the tempo of my flailing limbs to the smooth syncopation being piped out over the sound system. The room was spinning. It could have been the booze.

But then again, it could have been the roller skates.

Gabe's heads-up over e-mail had led me to discover a personals ad planted for the entire extended staff of the *Chronicle*.

It seemed that once a semester they liked to hit a kitschy downtown sports center for midnight roller disco. I'd been so thrilled to be included in the outing—by Gabe, no less—that it hadn't occurred to me how truly frightening it could be to see half the *Chronicle* editors on wheels. John O'Shea, possibly emboldened by the added height gained from the skates, was whizzing across the floor in frantic loops. Megan, Anna, and a few of the features editors were huddled by the shoe check laughing, gossiping, and scarfing down pizza. Myself, I'd taken the opportunity to sidle up to Mitch Abley, assistant sports editor and Target #16. I'd been psyched, firstly because Mitch represented the halfway point for this semi-torturous game, and also because he was friendly and incredibly normal-seeming.

That was, until he put his skates on.

Poor Mitch had clearly never been big with the roller hockey. Since he'd suited up, we'd spent the better part of an hour inching along the perimeter of the rink, Mitch clutching the guardrail for dear life. The experience was mildly humiliating, even for those of us who were having no problem staying upright. I had to cross my fingers and pray that Gabe was too focused on doing his own thing (i.e., watching pro-figure skater Kyra bust out her perfect figure eights right down the middle of the rink) to notice me or my escort for the evening.

"So, I guess maybe it's disloyal or something, 'cause of how I'm from Philly, but I'm really into the Giants," Mitch was saying to me.

That was the other thing about Mitch. While, upon first contact, he seemed happy to make with the school-related small talk, once we'd exhausted those pleasantries, he'd launched straight into sportscaster mode, rattling off facts and statistics about different teams, leagues, managers, RBI, average yearly salaries, number of assists. . . . It wasn't helping with my head-spinning thing.

I glanced around. John O'Shea was on another speed bender, and Megan and Co. were headed to the bar for another round. All around me, it seemed, people were having normal, nonawkward, potentially interesting experiences and conversations. And meanwhile, I'd already done the target thing. Was it my fault that, like the fourteen endeavors before this, it had been a bust?

Mitch groped wildly at the wall and went down.

It was time to cut bait.

"Um, yeah, I guess I don't know so much about sports," I confessed, crouching down to help Mitch back to his feet.

"Well, there's a basketball game at the Fleet Center on Saturday that I'm covering for the paper, if you'd, ah, like to come," Mitch said, blushing furiously.

I let go of his hand and flipped backward with a thud, landing on my butt. "Oh . . . ," I started. "That's, um, really cool of you to invite me, but, uh . . ." I drew a blank. There was no *way* I was going out with Roller Boy to watch basketball. I mean, basketball was a tall order—even for someone I *liked.*

Suddenly I remembered. "My ex is coming next weekend!" I said triumphantly. It was perfect: It was true, it was inarguable and, best of all, it suggested a certain romantic unavailability.

"Hey guys, how's the weather down there?"

Suddenly long arms were stretched around my waist from behind me, lifting me up off of the ground. Once I was standing, the arms made their way to my hips and spun me around.

"Um, thanks, Gabe, you're a lifesaver," I said, mortified.

Gabe sank down onto his knees and grabbed Mitch by the wrists, slowly springing back upward and effectively dragging Mitch with him.

Back in an upright position, Mitch dusted himself off with his hands and tried to regain some of his composure. "Thanks, man," he said to Gabe. "We were drowning out there." He turned back to me. "Well, if you want to catch a game some other time—you know, some weekend when your boyfriend's not in town—just let me know."

He turned to skate off, sailing away in short, staccato bursts while groping at the handrail. The drama of his delivery was undercut slightly by the *clutch-inch-clutch-inch* pacing of his departure, but I got the gist: a man scorned.

I turned back to Gabe. "I hate sports," I said, as though I owed him some sort of explanation for the awkwardness of that encounter.

Gabe peered at me. "Your *boyfriend's* coming this weekend?"

"No, I mean, he is. But he's not my boyfriend. He's my ex. Drew. My ex-Drew. You remember the picture," I said, babbling.

Gabe nodded slowly. "Right, the one from your wallet." He paused. "Cool."

"Yeah." I shrugged. "Yeah."

Suddenly the DJ's voice filled the sound system, layering over the music. "Everybody! Grab a partner! It's time for couples-skate!"

Gabe looked at me awkwardly. I looked away. I looked at him awkwardly. He looked away. Just as we threatened to combust with the force of our combined tension, Kyra glided over on gilded wheels, flaxen hair trailing out behind her. She gracefully came to a spinning stop just between Gabe and me, forcing me to jerk back a pace.

"You don't mind if I borrow him, hon, do you?" she asked me sweetly.

I shook my head. "Of course not."

She linked an elbow through his and pushed off and away. I watched them for a beat, then slowly skated off, away from the rink floor.

Seven

from: gflynn12@woodmanuniv.edu
to: cbclarkson@woodmanuniv.edu
re: this weekend

Hey, Claudia—

I looked for you at the roller disco last night after couples-skate, but I guess you'd already left? I was thinking about how you've got a guest this weekend, and I wanted to offer you some tickets. Mad Salad is playing at the Tin Room Saturday night. I don't know what kind of music Drew's into, but they're pretty much easy-listening. Think The Strokes. Rock all the way. I bet he'd like it.

Anyway, maybe you've already got your own thing planned, but I wanted to put it out there. The passes are down at the paper. If you want them, they're yours. And you wouldn't have to cover the show, or anything, since you'll probably be too busy entertaining to write.

Just lemme know.

—G

9/20, 2:17 p.m.
from: cbclarkson@woodmanuniv.edu
to: gflynn12@woodmanuniv.edu
re: re: this weekend

Yeah, sorry about the disappearing act. I got really tired all of a sudden and just had to split. Was up late the night before studying and I guess it caught up to me.

Anyway, that's really cool of you about the tix. I'd love to take them—if you're sure it's okay. And I can write it up, no worries. I know you're always looking to fill the page and stuff.

Thanks again. You rock.

—xx

9/20, 2:44 p.m.
from: gflynn12@woodmanuniv.edu
to: cbclarkson@woodmanuniv.edu
re: re: re: this weekend

No big, babe. Glad to hook you up.
Ain't that what friends are for?

;)

9/21, 7:22 p.m.
from: cbclarkson@woodmanuniv.edu
to: kissandtellen@shemail.net,
clnorton@woodmanuniv.edu
re: Just call me Suzie Samaritan

There I was this afternoon, walking back uphill after women's history. I was stopped at a street corner when a cute little silver VW Jetta pulled up, heavy bass pumping from the windows, which were open. I stepped back to let the car continue on, but it didn't move. I assumed the driver was letting me cross, so I set forth, but as I passed in front of the car, I could see that the driver was in fact a boy about my age, alone. He was struggling with a map and looking confused.

Hey, now, I thought. *Looks like Target #17 to me.*

I leaned against the driver's side door, offering up a wide grin. "Can I help you find your way?" I asked, ever the friendly neighbor.

The boy looked up at me quizzically, but smiled when he realized what I was saying.

Then he shoved the map at me and began to shoot rapid-fire questions at me successively.

Not in English.

Not in Spanish.

Not in French.

Which basically covered it, as far as languages that I spoke, understood or, at the very least, recognized.

I rearranged my features in what I hoped was a gesture of contrition. I flashed my eyes at him: *So sorry, my mistake.* Judging from his own expression of supreme irritation, he got the picture.

Slowly but surely, I backed away from the car, waving my wayward tourist onward.

—xx

When I got home from classes the next evening, I could hear Madonna blaring through the closed door to my dorm room. This was a good sign. I knew that bids were being given out that day, and if Charlie was rocking *The Immaculate Collection,* it meant that she'd gotten one from Tri-Delt.

I pushed the door open. "I take it we've got good news?" I asked, shouting to be heard above the music.

Charlie shrieked and ran at me. She picked me up and twirled me around. "You bet!" she shouted, giggling. "I got my bid! I'm going to be a Tri-Delt!"

"That's awesome," I gushed. "I guess all those nights of wearing ice-cream toppings to bed really paid off."

She pinched me. "Don't be jealous. It could have been you."

I nodded. "You're right. But something tells me you're going to pledge hard enough for the both of us. Let me see your bid."

She slid under her bed and pulled out a shoe box. "Here it is. I started a collection for my sorority scrapbook. I wanted to have a record of the whole entire experience." She smiled dreamily.

Charlie showed me her bid and then told me in more detail about the pledge process. It seemed to involve debasing oneself and forgoing basic human comforts like food and sleep over the course of a month to prove loyalty to the sisterhood. But she was incredibly eager and excited, and I was happy for her.

"Hey—," I said, after the group hugs had subsided. "I have some news of my own. And actually it sort of involves you. Or rather, affects you."

"Share!" she commanded, sitting upright on her bed and facing me.

"Drew is coming this weekend."

"Oh, my god!" she shrieked. "This is huge! Are you nervous?"

I nodded. "Totally. I've sort of not been thinking about it this week, but yeah. He swears he's just here as a friend, but it's gonna be weird, for sure."

She looked at me suspiciously. "Are you sure you *want* him here just as a friend?"

"I'm not sure of anything," I admitted. "Even with this 'target practice'—I'm getting better at approaching guys, and all, but I'm still totally striking out with the follow-through."

"No dates?" she asked sympathetically.

"Not a one. Not unless you count the delivery guy from Mexicali Rose. And he was, like, forty. Not so much my type."

"And that guy from the paper who asked you to the basketball game," Charlie pointed out helpfully.

"Oh, yeah," I said, remembering. "It just goes to show how excited I was about that. Not. Anyway: Drew. It should be interesting."

"Just go with the flow," Charlie advised.

"That's the plan," I agreed. "I don't really see a better way to handle it."

"Do you want me to crash in Shelley's room while he's here?" she offered.

"Yes. No. I have no idea," I said miserably.

Charlie leaned over and hugged me. "That's okay. We can just play it by ear. If you need moral support or some sort of buffer, I'll stay. If you need QT with your ex-honey, I'll go. Either way."

"You're the best, Charlie," I said, meaning it. "I promise I won't make fun of your sorority scrapbook ever again."

"But you didn't make fun of it," she protested.

"In my head I did, a little," I said guiltily. "Sorry."

She giggled. "I don't care. Mock all you want. I'm going to be a Tri-Delt!" She jumped up to her feet again and got her groove back on with Madonna.

There was a knock at the door, but Charlie was too immersed in a newly patented butt-shimmy to pay it any mind.

"Don't worry about that, I'll just answer the door myself," I said teasingly. Charlie pretended not to hear me.

I opened the door to find myself face-to-face with a giant bouquet of balloons. I jumped backward.

"CONGRATULATIONS!" the balloons shouted at me.

I turned to Charlie. "I think the talking balloons must be for you," I said.

"Goody!" she exclaimed, leaping daintily across the room. "Bring 'em on!"

A shiny-faced boy of the freshman variety crossed our threshold and dropped to one knee. "The sisters of Delta Delta Delta are thrilled that you have decided to accept their pledge bid," he said ceremoniously, extending the balloons.

"This is so exciting!" Charlie squealed, grabbing the balloons out of his hand and incorporating them into her dance routine.

Between the balloons that ate Boston, the blaring music, and the boy who looked like he might actually *combust* of nervousness, I was starting to feel a little bit claustrophobic. I took my own personal soul train out into the hallway for some air.

9/22, 6:32 p.m.
from: cbclarkson@woodmanuniv.edu
to: kissandtellen@shemail.net
re: Optimism in the face of rejection?

Well, Ells, Charlie got her pledge bid this afternoon—and *also* the most gi-normous bouquet of balloons I've ever seen, delivered via Freaked-out Frosh. When I stepped outside to give him some space, I stepped into Target #18. Unlike his Freaked-out Frosh Friend, however, though, this dude didn't seem nervous. Only irritated.

"Hey!" I said. "Are you part of the balloon squad?"

He shot me a look of pure death. "No, that's my buddy's gig. I just promised him I'd take him around because I'm the one with wheels."

"You're a good man," I said brightly. "The world needs more of your generosity."

Scowl-boy wasn't biting. "Whatever," he said, fiddling with his car keys and steadfastly refusing to meet my gaze.

"Look, you know, you don't have to hang out in the hall," I said, strangely compelled to press on. "Target practice" had that effect on me. "I mean, it's pretty crowded in there—Madonna herself takes up at least ninety percent of the square footage—but we can squeeze. The more, the merrier!"

He sighed heavily. "Just tell Cal I'm gonna wait in the car," he grumbled, pivoting and making tracks down the hallway.

"I sure will!" I said, feeling foolish.

I mean, what is the deal, anyway? Just when I think that I may have managed to grasp the slightest purchase on dealing with the opposite sex, someone like scowl-boy comes along and makes me feel the size of a jelly bean. And infinitely less appealing than a jelly bean, as well.

Maybe I shouldn't even bother with this game. It hasn't been all that much fun.

Whatever. What do I care? I have other things to worry about. Drew is coming tomorrow, after all. And with eighteen targets down, the game is going to have to be put on hold for the weekend. It's the only way, I figure, to preserve what little sanity I have left.

—xx

Eight

South Station was an assault on each of my senses: The stench of exhaust fumes mixed with the sharply sweet scent of baked goods from chain cafés, and thick, fuzzy announcements blared dully over the blurred roar of the commuters wandering through the terminal. I felt panicky and overwhelmed by it all.

Of course, the anticipation of seeing Drew might well have been the primary cause of my anxiety. I hadn't laid eyes on him since the night before he left for Columbia. That had been at least four weeks ago. Since we'd started dating, we'd never gone a whole month without seeing each other. Not even during summers. If one of us traveled, we were generally back within the month. Or if one of us was away working, the other visited on weekends. In short, we'd been permanent fixtures in each other's lives over the last three years. But then, that was when we'd been dating. Everything was different now.

And what about Drew? Would *he* be different? Taller? Thinner? Would he have changed his hair? I really hoped not. I always liked his clean-cut, preppy look. Drew had always been steady. Reliable. But maybe in college he'd become some kind of crazed party animal. Maybe he'd been dating. It was hard for me to imagine, but then again, I'm sure Drew never imagined me engaged in anything like "target practice." So it was probably best not to make any assumptions. Just "go with the flow," as Charlie had suggested.

I wasn't feeling very flow-y.

I took a deep breath and hitched up my jeans. I was wearing my expensive pair, and I'd taken the time to do my hair wavy, the way Drew liked it. I had no idea what to expect when he came off the bus, but I wanted him to like what he saw. We had broken up on good terms; I had no clue as to what that would mean for our weekend together.

I glanced at my watch. He was three minutes late. Three minutes, and I was starting to unravel. *Get a grip, Claudia,* I thought, closing my eyes for a moment and forcing myself to take deep, steady breaths.

"Am I interrupting a Zen moment?"

My eyes flew open, and sure enough, there he was. "Drew!" I shrieked, enveloping him in a huge bear hug.

"Hey, Bee," he whispered, burying his face in my hair. I didn't care how much time had passed; nothing at all had changed. Holding Drew, it felt as though we were standing on his front porch the night before he left for school. I clung to him, nostalgia washing over me in powerful waves.

After a moment, Drew stepped back. "I hate to break this up, but I think we have to get out of here, like now. That weird guy behind the condiments rack's been eyeing my backpack, and I just don't like the looks of him."

I laughed. "Good call."

He reached out and put his hands on my shoulders. "You do look great, Claud. Really fabulous."

"Thanks," I said shyly. "You too." And he did: tall, broad-shouldered, muscular. Just like his normal self, his sandy brown hair scruffy and his blue eyes full of warmth. And yet, the time apart made him appear to me to be his *best* self, slightly more mature in an indefinable way. I couldn't pinpoint it or define how I was feeling. This was Drew, the person who understood me fully, the person with whom I was wholly comfortable, and wholly myself. So seeing him was like slipping into my favorite pair of pajamas: welcoming, comfortable. I wanted to wrap him around me for the duration of the weekend, to drown in his familiar presence.

But he wasn't my boyfriend anymore— I had to remind myself of that. And that basic truth reset the playing field and made me feel insecure.

He must have felt it, too, because suddenly his hands were dangling awkwardly at his sides. "Well, which way to the T?" he asked, overcompensating for the moment with exaggerated enthusiasm.

I gestured. "It's an easy ride. We're right off the Red line."

Drew grabbed his bag and followed me down the corridor.

Seeing Drew in the bus station was the emotional equivalent of a ride on the Tilt-A-Whirl: exhilarating, yes, but completely discombobulating, too. And yet, it took only a moment for us to hug hello, and suddenly it was just like old times.

That is, if old times had been awkward and tentative.

The thing is that we knew each other inside out, and so there was no way, really, to completely step back from that. But at the same time, there was this huge, honking elephant in the room with us, otherwise known as our breakup. And one minute I wanted to jump into his lap, kiss him, and have everything be just like it was for the past four years.

And then I remembered "target practice," and cool people like that guy Dave, or my friend Brett from comp sci—and

Gabe, can't forget Gabe. But *then* I remembered that Gabe's with Kyra, and that nothing ever happened with Dave or Brett. And that most of my targets have fled from me screaming. (Literally. Screaming. I mean, do you have any idea what that does to the ego?) And I just don't know what the answer is.

Anyway, we came back to my dorm making normal, polite-person conversation. I guess we had both decided that we were going to try to keep things on a healthy, nonweird level—at least for as long as we could. And I walked him around campus and showed him all of my favorite places, like making him try the flavored coffee syrups at Brew and Gold. He liked Woodman, saying that it was "refreshing" to be on an actual campus as opposed to a network of buildings that had been just sort of plunked down into the middle of a city.

We decided to go into Cambridge for dinner. Drew was tired and not up for heading back downtown, and, anyway, Harvard Square is really lively on a Friday night, and very quaint. We hit this great

Indian restaurant I'd found. Drew had never tried Indian food before, so I got to order him one of those huge samplers and we both just gorged and laughed and drank lots of cheap wine despite our lack of IDs (real or fake). It was perfect. And easy. And comfortable.

From there we stopped by one of the few local dive bars that didn't bother to card. We grabbed a table in the corner, and Drew got us some beers. The minute we sat down, though, I could tell he was having thoughts of the serious variety.

"So," he began, "I think we need to talk."

I immediately clapped my hands over my ears in protest. "No way. Nothing good in the history of conversation has ever come from those words."

He laughed. "Relax, Claud. I just want to be honest with you. You should know why I came out here."

"You wanted to surprise me," I reminded him. "Just like Buji's girlfriend was surprising him. It was a chain reaction of surprises."

"Well, yes," he said, "but it's more than

that. I probably would have come out here even if Buji hadn't been hosting a weekend of love in our swinging bachelor pad. I wanted to see you. I've really missed you, Bee."

"I've missed you too," I admitted quietly, glancing down at the chipped wooden table. I wondered about all of the kids my age who'd been at this table before me, and how many of them had had "talks" like ours. Or talks of any kind. I wondered how many other people in the bar were on complicated dates, trying to navigate the course of relationships as they took their first steps toward independence. I bet there were a lot of us. We should have started a support group or something. God knows I could have used one.

Drew reached across the table and took my hand in his. "Bee, I have to say this: I still love you."

My voice caught in my throat, and I looked away.

He stretched his free hand over and gently redirected me so that we were face-to-face again. "I still love you, and I want to be with you. I understand why you wanted to try things apart, I understand that you wanted to start college on your own, but for me, I've had enough. I'm not interested in other girls, and being in separate schools is independence enough. If we still love each other—which, I think we do—then I don't know why we can't be together. I know it's distance, but it's not like Africa distance. It's four hours on the bus. The very reasonably priced bus. And I think we're giving up too easily on something very special." He paused and took a sip of his beer.

I realized that it was my turn to say something. "I, uh . . . I really don't know what to say, Drew."

His expression crumbled, and he pulled his hand back into his lap. "Do you not love me anymore?"

I shook my head slowly. "Of course. That's not it, Drew. I've loved you for four years. Four weeks of separation isn't going to undo that. And of course I think about you, and about what we had, and about maybe . . . being with you again. I'm tempted. I'm definitely tempted. But I'm not sure, honestly, that it's the right decision."

"Is there someone else?" he asked, his voice low.

"*No.* Definitely not. And even if there were, I wouldn't be just . . . *replacing* you so soon after things ended. But maybe . . . maybe the point of college is to break out of your comfort zone, to try to stand on your own two feet."

"You need a support system, Claud," he protested.

"That's true. I get that. And thank god I have that. You, Ellen . . . you've been great. And like I said, no one I meet here will ever replace any of you. But you both are one part of me, and school is another. And I think I need to spend more time figuring out what, exactly, school *is* to me before I can let worlds collide and overlap." I looked up at him nervously. "Does that make sense?"

He sighed. "Unfortunately, it does. It's not the answer I was hoping for, but I get you. But just promise me this."

"What?"

"Just promise me that you won't make any decisions right this minute. Let's take the weekend to be together, no pressure, just like old times. And then we can see where we are on Sunday. Does that make sense? I mean, we owe it to ourselves to at least be open-minded."

I considered his words and decided he had a point. Besides, at that moment all I wanted to do was wrap myself around him and disappear for a few days. So this did seem like a fair compromise.

"I promise," I said.

Drew was as good as his word. When he finally woke on Saturday at noon, groggy from beer and fragmented sleep, he slipped back into comfort-mode. He slid out of bed and into the shower, with a quick kiss on the forehead for me, but without any mention of our conversation of the previous night. I adored him for that.

After we'd both dressed, we headed to the town center for brunch. I wanted him to see the local culture. Then we hit downtown Boston. Drew was completely charmed by the picturesque brownstones that lined the side streets of the shopping district. I indulged his sporting goods thing, and he was good-natured about my need to try on six thousand different pairs of shoes (of which, I am proud to report, I only bought one). We even stopped in at the Institute of Contemporary Art, which was actually sort of above our heads, I am sorry to say. We splurged on seafood for dinner at a place that used actual table-cloths. Drew ordered us each a glass of champagne and when they arrived, we clinked glasses wordlessly. After dinner, we stole back to campus for a quick power nap, curling up tightly together on my narrow single bed for a half hour or so. And then it was time for the concert.

The Tin Room was exactly as I had remembered it, which, given that I'd nearly blacked out my entire first night there, was a good thing. (I mean, remembering *anything* about that night was really a triumph for me.) And Gabe had been right about Mad Salad: *très* listen-able. The main room was filled to capacity, and we squeezed our way across the floor with our stomachs sucked in.

"This band is awesome," Drew said, screaming directly into my ear. "How'd you hear about them?"

"My friend from the paper. He's the music editor," I said casually.

"Oh, that's right," Drew said, coming up behind me and wrapping his arms around my waist. "You're the cool arts writer with the connections."

It was stiflingly hot in the room, and Drew's embrace suddenly felt suffocating. I shrugged him off as delicately as possible.

"What's wrong?" he asked, not fooled for a minute.

"I, uh—do you want to get a drink?" I stammered.

Drew shrugged. "Sure. Where's the bar?"

That, I remembered. I grabbed his hand and tugged him in the direction of the back room, weaving our way through drunken rockers. "Two pints, please," I shouted, nodding at the bartender.

"Hey, it's you," the bartender said, smiling. "Upchuck Betty."

"*Huh?*" I said, appalled.

"I remember you, from the Rice and Beans show a couple of weeks ago. You tossed your cookies all over your boyfriend," he said, still with the grinning and not paying any mind to my growing expression of panic.

"Um, he was *not* my boyfriend," I hissed, praying that Drew was too engrossed in the music to hear our exchange. "He was my friend's friend!"

"It was freakin' hysterical, that's what it was," the bartender asserted. He slid two filled pint glasses, each frothy and foaming, down the bar toward me. "Now, sweetie, tonight our goal is to know when to say when, okay?" He winked.

I glared at him and thrust Drew's beer toward him. Then I took my own and sucked down half of it in one gulp, which did not go unnoticed by my new best friend, Creepy McBeerslinger.

"What the heck was *that* all about?" Drew asked, eyeing the bartender suspiciously. Apparently he *had* heard our conversation. "Did you pull a Coyote Ugly here sometime, or what?"

"Or what." I sighed. "I was here with Charlie, and we drank too much. Then she dragged over these annoying guys. But I was past the point of no return, and in my inebriated state I mistook one of them for a toilet bowl. . . . It wasn't pretty."

Drew chuckled, but it was a hollow sound and I suspected the bartender's unfortunate use of the term "boyfriend" had gotten to him. I decided to play dumb. Besides, I hadn't done anything wrong, anyway.

I lifted my beer to my lips again, but to my surprise, Drew covered the rim with his hand. "Easy there, 'Upchuck Betty,'" he said, borrowing my charming new nickname.

"Thanks, Dad," I snapped. What the hell? Since when was Drew so bossy? And when the *hell* had it gotten so cloying hot in here? "Let's just go listen to the band," I said flatly.

"Fine," Drew intoned, marching off through the crowd.

"Oh, look, it's, uh, the *feminist* chick again!"

Oh, god. What was this—scenes from my non-love life? I whirled around to see Cameron, meathead Troy's let's-get-physical friend, leering at me. "Hey, babe." He winked. "Did Troy tell you I was going to be here tonight?"

"Hardly," I said, frustrated. "He doesn't exactly keep me apprised of your comings-and-goings." Troy and Charlie were seeing each other pretty regularly, but we'd made a pact never again to mention our ill-fated double date.

Cameron shrugged, and shuffled his beefy body closer to my own. "What, you're too good for me? Please. Troy says he's seen you around, on campus, hitting on every guy you see. From what I understand, you're a little bit hard up. You should be thankful that I'm willing to give you a test run."

"Ew, I should think not," I said, shoving his hand off of me and stepping as far backward as I could, given the crush. "Don't you, like, go to Amherst? What are you even doing here?"

"I wouldn't miss a Mad Salad gig," he said, wrapping his free hand around my waist.

This was getting to be a little bit scary. The music was loud enough to drown out our conversation, and people were packed tightly against one another enough not to notice the fact of my being groped. All in all, it was a highly not-pleasant situation. One that I wasn't sure I knew how to side-step.

"What the f—"

I looked up, and suddenly, miraculously, Cameron was moving backward, apparently against his will.

"She's not interested, man. Let it go."

It was Drew. I thought I'd lost him to the wild thrashing going on in the main room, but here he was, my knight in shining Abercrombie. He grabbed at Cameron's shirt with both hands. "Get gone," he said gruffly.

Cameron paused and sized Drew up. The meathead did have about four inches on my ex. But there was something to the look in Drew's eye that made him think twice.

"Whatever. She's just a tease, man. I don't know what you're getting so worked up about. She's not worth it," Cameron grumbled.

"I mean it," Drew said. "Shut your mouth and walk away."

With one final sneer, Cameron slunk off as much as the crowd would allow.

I turned to Drew. "Thank you so much," I gushed. "I have no idea what was wrong with that freak. I mean, we met that one time, but *nothing* happened and he was *so* overreacting just now, and, like, no one even noticed what was going on——"

"We need to talk, Claudia," Drew said stiffly. It was the second time he'd said those words in as many days. I had a feeling this little conversation wouldn't include many proclamations of undying love, however. "Is there anyplace around here that's quiet?"

"Downstairs toward the bathrooms?" I guessed.

He led me to the lower level, which was all but empty this evening as there was no band playing on the second stage. We made our way down a rickety hallway to the general area of the bathroom. There was a small corridor off to the side that afforded us a slight bit of privacy and some distance from the bathroom "ambiance."

Once we'd semisequestered ourselves, Drew flashed me a look of utter despair. He was breathing heavily. This didn't bode well. Drew generally reserved his heavy breathing for moments of intense passion or fits of thinly repressed anger. So we were either going to make out, or he was about three sharp "ohms" away from going postal on me.

"What?" I said, hoping to stall for time and diffuse the situation somewhat.

"You tell me, Claudia," he said. "What the hell is going on?"

"*Nothing* is going on, Drew," I insisted. "Except for the fact that I ran into some people I know and you're totally freaking out."

"Yeah, I'm freaking out, because apparently the people that you 'know'"—he made sarcastic air quotes with his fingers—"are a bartender with cute nicknames pertaining to your alcoholic tendencies, and a stalker who's looking to sexually assault you in the middle of a concert! Who, by the way, *claims* to have been on a date with you? I mean, huh?"

"Well, okay, but it's not like I was *encouraging* either of them!" I shouted. The strain of being so close to Drew all weekend and not knowing where we stood, the pent-up emotions, and the incredible heat of the club were all pressing upon me. I was ready to combust.

"Well what's your deal, lately, that you're coming to bars and drinking until you puke on your date? I'd be upset, you know, that you're dating, but somehow I find it slightly more disturbing that you're *throwing up* on your dates! Or going around with guys who *clearly* have, shall we say, *expectations* of you? I mean, is this why you don't want to get back together? So you can puke on strange boys and beat off your more . . . aggressive suitors? Is *that* what your independence is all about?"

"My independence isn't *about* anything, Drew!" I yelled. "I told you yesterday that I love you, and I meant it. I'm not looking to replace you! But being here, being away, on my own, is a chance to figure out who *I* am, just me, without any more outside influences."

"So I'm an outside influence?" Drew asked, sounding appalled.

I lowered my voice. "In a good way," I said. "I promise. But there's a reason we each went to different colleges. We have different interests, and different sides of our personalities that we need to develop. We owe that to ourselves. I'm not saying this isn't hard, or that I don't miss you—of *course* I miss you. But we made promises to ourselves and to each other, and I just think it's too soon to recant."

Drew shook his head sadly, uncomprehending. "I don't get you, Claud," he said. "I understand wanting to come up to Boston, try out a new scene. But I don't see why that means tossing aside everything we had."

"It's not—"

"And don't tell me it's not, because it *is*. You could be here, doing your own thing, and I could be at Columbia, but we could still be, you know, *us*. Together. But you'd rather . . ." He trailed off, gesturing ambiguously in the direction of the bathroom. "You'd rather be binge drinking with strange boys than be my girlfriend. And I guess *that*, really, is where we're different." He paused. "Because I can do my thing and still be with you."

I looked at him, chin hanging practically to his chest. He looked so defeated. I wanted to pull him close to me, to stroke his hair, but I knew that wasn't the answer. He was right: We didn't want the same things. And therefore I didn't have anything to offer him.

"I'm gonna go," he said, finally.

"But—I have to—"

"You can stay," he said. "You *should* stay. I think I need a little bit of time to myself."

"Drew, I can't let you go back to campus all by yourself," I protested. That would have made me officially the Worst Ex-Girlfriend of the Year.

"Seriously, I want to," he said. "We've taken that stupid shuttle enough times already this weekend that I could find my way back in my sleep. Just let me go back and relax for a little bit. Cool off."

"If that's what you really want," I said, dubious.

"It is," he assured me. "Come on, Claudia. If you follow me home, we're just in for another two hours of awkward silence."

"You have a point," I admitted. It was annoying how Drew was always so logical. "But do you really think time apart will help you?"

"Let's put it this way: It couldn't hurt."

"Okay," I said. "In that case, you go and I'll be home in an hour or two." I fished my dorm key out of my back pocket and held it out to him. "Take this. But you'd better let me in when I get home."

He laughed. "I swear. After all, won't I need your meal card in the morning?"

I rolled my eyes. "Go. Now."

He turned and loped up the stairs slowly. I leaned against the wall and watched him go, feeling a mixture of confusion, resignation, and plain old sorrow. Maybe Drew was right. Maybe "finding myself" was just some sort of euphemism for acting out a scene from *College Girls Gone Wild.* I mean, since when was a yak-o-rama my own personal declaration of self? Sheesh.

I sighed.

"Wow, I think that's pretty much the sound of the weight of the world."

I looked up. It was Gabe, looking concerned.

Huh?

"I'm just having a—what are you doing here?" I asked.

"I love Mad Salad. Wouldn't miss it," he said. He put his hand on my forearm. "I kind of overheard your argument. I'm really sorry you guys aren't getting along."

"You *overheard* us?"

He jerked his head in the direction of the bathroom. "I had to go. And then, you know . . . with the cat. And the curiosity." He gazed at me with bemused interest. "Did you really puke on a date?"

"It wasn't a date!" I said irritably. "It was a friend of a friend of Charlie's."

"But the barfing . . . ," he prompted.

"Sad, but true."

Gabe burst out laughing. "I'm sorry, but that's totally classic."

I tried to stay frozen in irritable-mode, but Gabe's laughter was infectious. Besides, it had been a really long night.

There was something off, though, about seeing Gabe at the concert. Something that didn't feel quite right. At first, I couldn't put my finger on it. But then I realized. "But Gabe," I said, "if you love Mad Salad so much, why'd you offer your tickets to me? I mean, you could have used them. You *should* have used them."

"Well, I mean, I just . . ." He looked down and began to toy with a nonexistent piece of lint on his shirt. "It seemed like it'd be good for you. Something to do with Drew. You seemed nervous about the visit," he said finally.

I stared at him, struck by his response. How incredibly thoughtful and considerate it was of him to not only suggest an outing for me, knowing that I was going to have a guest, but to offer me his tickets and inconvenience himself. It was generous to the point of being odd. I didn't quite know what to say.

"Wow," I said finally. "That's . . . that was really thoughtful of you. I'm sorry you had to go buy yourself another set of tickets. I mean, since you're a fan and stuff."

He shrugged. "Not a problem. Glad to help out. I know it can be really awkward when the exes come to town."

"Let me make it up to you," I offered. "I could buy you a drink."

He wagged a finger at me. "No way, young lady. That way leads to messy endings. I know your nickname, after all."

I groaned. "*Please* don't tell anyone at the *Chronicle* about this?"

He held his hand up, a Boy Scout taking an oath.

"Tell them about what?"

I looked up, and thought, *I should have known.*

Standing next to Gabe and beaming brightly ahead was Kyra.

I tiptoed anxiously up the stairs to my dorm room, stepping around drunken couples giggling in the hallways. The building felt deserted despite the fact that I could hear movement and hushed whispering from behind closed doors. I reached the front door of my room and hesitated, nervous to enter, nervous to see Drew. I rapped on the door lightly, half-hoping he wouldn't answer, though I didn't know exactly what I'd do if he didn't.

Of course, Drew hadn't locked me out. He opened the door a crack, then pulled it back fully. The room was pitch-black, sharply divided by the shaft of light ushered in by the open door. Drew was wearing his boxers and a T-shirt, and his close-trimmed hair stood up from his head in sleep-sculpted spikes and peaks. His eyes were half-closed. He pulled me inside and closed the door quickly.

I glanced over at Charlie's still-made bed. "Where is she?" I whispered, as though afraid she was sleeping under her bed, or in her closet.

He indicated to a note taped to my computer monitor: *Sleeping at Shell's. See you in the morning?*

Oh.

Drew crawled back into my bed and burrowed under the covers. I stood, unsure, in the middle of the room. Given the night we'd just had, maybe the right thing to do would be to crash in Charlie's bed until morning? But . . . the rumpled sheets where Drew had cocooned himself were infinitely inviting. And my conscience had apparently gone AWOL. It was *Drew*, after all. And he was here, in my bed. And I didn't know when or if we'd have another chance to be together this way.

Soundlessly, I stepped out of my clothing, letting them fall to the floor. I slid between the sheets and draped one leg over

Drew, pulling myself into the negative space carved out by his chest. As I touched him, his eyes flew open in surprise. I reached out my hand and covered them again. He smiled. It was all the encouragement I needed. I leaned over and kissed him. And then he was kissing me back, holding me, as though nothing had changed.

And for that moment, for that night, nothing had. We were together, would always be together, emotionally connected if nothing else. We would always have this memory. I knew that, in the morning, things would be different; we would both have to face the need to move on. But morning wasn't for another few hours yet, and until it came, all I wanted was Drew.

Morning did come, of course, and with it the harsh glare of sunlight, sharp after a night tempered by alcohol, high emotion, and slow, hazy sex. I woke up before Drew, early, to find him pressed against me, spooning me from behind. His arm was firmly cinched around my waist, and he was breathing heavy, even breaths. I could feel his chest rise and fall. Carefully, so as not to wake him, I flipped myself around so that I was facing him. I ran my fingers over his face lightly, tracing his features, committing them to memory. I didn't regret our actions one bit, but I knew that the moment he woke up, the magic of those in-between hours would be broken. We'd be back in real time, facing the fact that he was going back to New York, and that I was not going to be his girlfriend anymore.

He peeled one eye open slowly, as if sensing my gaze. "Hi," he said softly.

"Hi," I replied, snuggling closer to him.

"What time is it?"

"Still early," I said. "You don't have to get up."

"I have a train," he reminded me. "I need to be back in the city in time for that study session."

Don't go, I thought wildly. *Stay here. You can live in the dorm with Charlie and me—she won't mind. You can transfer.* But I pushed those thoughts aside. They were knee-jerk ideas, not true to what I knew to be best.

Reading my thoughts, he leaned forward and kissed me. "Thanks for having me this weekend."

I smiled. "Surprise."

He touched my face lightly, and we kissed some more. "I didn't mean for this to happen," he said. "I mean, I was hoping you would consider getting back together, but I didn't, you know, have a plan—"

"It's fine," I said. "More than fine. It's what I wanted. I think it's what we both needed. Right?"

"Are you saying we slept together because we needed closure?" he asked carefully.

"Not exactly," I corrected. "It's more than that. There's much more emotion to it. But that's a part of it, don't you think?"

"Maybe," he conceded. "But whatever the reason, I'm glad we had a chance." He hugged me tightly. "You know I love you."

I nodded. "I love you too," I said. I struggled to keep the tears that threatened to spill down my cheeks at bay. Crying would not help this situation.

"I'm going to pack up," he said, "and then I'm going to hop that shuttle again for South Station. So I'll be out of your hair as soon as I can get my stuff together."

"It's okay," I protested. Now that he was actually leaving, all of my resolve had turned to dust. "You can stay in my hair as long as—"

"Claudia, I need to go," he said, pressing a finger to my lips gently. "And you need me to go."

We rose, and Drew showered quickly. I tossed the bedspread back down and messily centered myself on it, Indian-style, throw pillows cradled in my lap, watching him pack and offering small nuggets of mundane conversation. But really, there was little more to say. Finally, he had finished, and there was no more putting off his departure.

"Okay," he said, standing stiffly and holding his duffel in one tightly clenched fist.

"Okay," I said, pushing aside the small mountain of bedding I'd amassed, and rising.

"Look, Claudia, I'm not angry. I understand why you need things to be this way," he said.

"Do you really?"

He shrugged. "I'm not going to lie. Seeing firsthand just what exactly your 'independence' consists of wasn't, you know, the most fun I've ever had. I'm sure you'd feel the same way if you were in my position. But I respect you—I've always respected you, and I want you to be able to experience your first year at college just the way you want to."

"I really appreciate that," I said.

"There's always the future," he offered.

"Drew—," I said.

"I'm kidding. Sort of. The point is, never say never. You do your thing, and I'll do mine. And if we're meant to be together again, I'm sure we will be."

He was right. Which only made the reality of the situation that much more vivid to me. "I guess we won't be talking so much?" I asked.

"Well, I am *always* here for you. You can come to me anytime, with anything," he said. "But I think we both know that the best way to move on is, well . . . to move on."

"Who are you, and what have you done with Drew?" I teased.

"I had some time to myself last night," he reminded me. "It was good for me."

"I should leave you alone more often," I joked, realizing as I said it that I *would*, in fact, be leaving him alone more often, from now on. It was a sobering thought.

Drew must have sensed the shift in atmosphere as well. He dropped his bag and moved to me, taking me in his arms. He took my face in his hands and kissed me on the forehead. "We'll be okay," he said. "I promise."

I nodded, and walked him to the door. One last "I love you, Bee," and he was gone.

It wasn't until I was back in bed, swaddled with pillows, sheets, and blankets again, that I let myself cry. I curled into as tight of a ball as I could manage and let loose, letting go of all of the frustration, tension, and bittersweet pain of the past two days. When I was done, I closed my eyes and slept.

It was Charlie who found me four hours later, still in sweats, still in bed. She took one look at me and called in for pizza. "We'll just have a girl's night, you and me," she said. "I'll do your nails. Does that sound good?"

I nodded weakly. "Don't you have a pledge event?" She always did, it seemed.

"I think there's another sister who needs me tonight," she said, jumping into bed next to me and giving me a squeeze.

"Thank you," I said. It was all I could manage.

Nine

**LOCAL STUDENTS GET TOSSED
AT THE TIN ROOM
Mad Salad Rocks the House
on Saturday Night**

Mix one part the raw, stripped-down essence of the White Stripes with two parts the crowd-pleasing listenability of Maroon 5, throw in a front man with more sex appeal than Usher. Shake, don't stir, and you've got Mad Salad. More than that, you've got the reason why the Tin Room rocked to the rafters this weekend.

Indeed, though the bulk of the

audience was students from the greater Boston area, some in the crowd had traveled from far-flung Williams, Amherst, and beyond, just to have their salads tossed.

The band did not disappoint. They played nearly every song from their most recent release, *Eat Your Vegetables*, as well as drew from their insanely popular debut album, *Five Servings a Day.*

The band members, friends dating back to elementary school, were happy to sit down with the *Chronicle* for a quick chat.

"Oh, yeah, we just love playing Boston," lead singer Kyle Merrin said, pausing briefly to tune a guitar. "The college kids—they're our core fan base."

"Yeah, Boston rules!" drummer Trent Billie chimed in. "We were just down in New York, and let me tell you, those crowds get ugly. We were, like, not feeling the love down there!" He leaned

forward and lowered his voice.
"They throw stuff."

9/26, 10:02 p.m.
from: cbclarkson@woodmanuniv.edu
to: clnorton@woodmanuniv.edu,
kissandtellen@shemail.net
re: Rock stars are . . .

 . . . different from you and me. But my interview with Mad Salad knocks four more targets off of my list.

Gabe let slide the fact of my being twenty-
four hours late with a story that ended up
being more pre-fab than fab. I assured him
I'd done my best (leaving out the part
where I'd had to cut the interview short
after the bassist—the *married* bassist—
propositioned me). I'd e-mailed the article
to him and then spent the better part of the
evening in the library. I'd made a serious
dent in my outline for the pop culture essay
and was feeling pretty proud of myself. I
gathered my books and wandered outside
for some fresh air. The roof of the library
offered a gorgeous view of campus and,
beyond, downtown Boston. As such, it was

the site of many a smoking break and confessions of undying love. I, of course, just wanted to stretch my legs.

"Hey, Claud!"

I turned to see Charlie walking up the steps to the roof. She was a little bit overdressed for a random Monday night, swathed in tailored wool pants, polished, heeled boots, and a cashmere sweater set. "Where ya been?" I asked, indicating the ensemble. That's what it was, really. An *ensemble.* I was suddenly aware of how long it had been since I'd washed my jeans.

She pointed. "At the house."

"The House" meant the Tri-Delt mansion, located just one block parallel to fraternity row.

"I should have just assumed," I teased. "Good night?"

As a pledging sister, Charlie was often sworn to secrecy about many of the goings-on of the process. This was for the most part okay with me, except for those moments when I could tell she wanted to talk. This was one of the moments. The *dying for a cigarette* look on her face was a dead giveaway (she'd been a chimney in junior high, she told me, but had had to give it up when the pageant circuit kicked into high gear).

She shrugged. "Yeah, it was fun. I mean, it was nice."

I frowned, not sure of the difference between the two and not wanting to pry. Fortunately, Charlie was feeling talkative. "We got our big sisters tonight."

"Oh, cool!" I said. This was, like, a thing, I knew. Each pledge was paired up with an older sister who would look out for her and guide her through the process. It was all about mentoring and fostering friendship. Which, in that case—why did Charlie look so miserable? "Not cool?"

She sighed deeply. "Anu Shah is my big sister."

I raised an eyebrow.

"She goes out with Zach Masters?"

"Still not ringing a bell."

She crossed her arms over her chest. "Well, perhaps that's because the first time you met them you were so drunk on Cosmopolitans that you basically threw yourself at Zach!"

Oh, *Zach*. Sure. I remembered him.

President of the Inter-Greek Council, no? His girlfriend was pretty pissed. . . . "Oh, Charlie," I said, realizing.

"Yeah."

"But, I mean, *you* weren't the one throwing yourself at Zach that night. It was totally me! I don't think you were even anywhere near me in the room!"

"Judging from the way that Anu was behaving tonight, I'm not sure that matters."

"But I thought the big sisters got to pick their own little sisters. I mean, she wouldn't have picked you if she hated you, right?"

"It's not an exact science," Charlie explained, shaking her head. "There are a certain number of upperclassmen who sign up to be big sisters. They put in their requests, but it doesn't always work out. So I don't know. But based on the looks she was shooting me all through our ceremony, I'd say she isn't thrilled about this matchup."

"I'm sure you're just being paranoid," I said, even though I wasn't. Charlie was a frighteningly good judge of character. If she thought this chick was pissed at her, then the chick probably was.

Charlie shrugged. "Whatever. There's

nothing I can do about it now, anyway, right? I guess the trick is to be Super-pledge. Make sure she doesn't have any reason to dislike me."

"Well, that shouldn't be too hard," I said. "I mean, you already *were* Super-pledge."

"We'll see," she said worriedly.

I didn't like the tone in her voice. It was one I'd never heard before. Charlie didn't normally get rattled by social situations and the like.

"Charlie, I am so sorry," I said. "Honestly, it was just me being stupid, trying to prove to myself that I was capable of talking to boys. Which, clearly, I am not, given the stupid chain reaction of events I seem to have set into motion."

"No way," Charlie protested. "Anu's being a freak. My friend hit on her friend's boyfriend—unknowingly—a month ago? Please."

"Good point. But you still have to make with the nice."

Charlie leveled me with her patented *Are you kidding?* look. "Do you really think I wouldn't?"

"Of course not!" I insisted, wrapping my

arm around her. Her thin frame felt frail to my touch. "Enough of this sad pondering," I insisted. "The yogurt shop's still open."

At this, she perked up slightly. "Your treat?" she asked playfully.

I groaned. "I guess I owe you."

"Oh, Claudia." She sighed wistfully. "You're like the big sister I never had."

9/28, 12:38 p.m.
from: cbclarkson@woodmanuniv.edu
to: clnorton@woodmanuniv.edu,
kissandtellen@shemail.net
re: Good morning and happy lunchtime!

Hola, Chicas—

Just coming from the comp sci lab. Always an invigorating way to start the day. But today I come bearing good tidings. For starters, Hartridge (who seems to like me better now that I'm wearing pants and coming to class on time) has graciously offered to let those of us who failed that last quiz turn in some extra credit. Which is a shame, really, for all those kids who were cruising straight to A-ville on the basis of my contribution to the curve. But no complaints here. At this point I'd be thrilled to make a swift pit stop over to D-town.

Of course, with every rainbow comes just a little bit of rain, mainly in the form of my own semipublic humiliation.

After several weeks of smiling shyly at Jesse and hoping he'd managed to get the espresso out of his pants, I decided to step up the flirt level. I knew, technically, that talking to Jesse wasn't the same thing as approaching someone entirely new, but the fact was that as my own skills evolved, so, I believed, should the game. Meaning that I was ready to progress with Jesse beyond the hasty "Whoops—sorry!" I'd originally offered.

I was ready to ask him out.

And the announcement regarding the extra credit gave me just the opportunity to do so.

I wanted to talk to him after class, but he seemed to have other ideas. He went up to the front of the room and started an insanely long diatribe with Hartridge about coded matrices. I wondered furtively if I was supposed to know what those things were. No matter. If Jesse was actually *good* at comp sci, then instead of offering to work together, I'd just ask him to tutor me. See? Easy-peasy. I was a master adapter, proficient in the Art of the Flirt.

As the moments dragged on, it became increasingly difficult to pretend that I had any reason to be lingering in the lab. Finally, I grabbed my bag and made my way into the hall. I stalled rather impressively—checking my cell, consulting my PDA, looking over my list of reading for bio. . . . I was halfway through creating a new iPod playlist when Jesse finally emerged from the classroom.

"Hey!" I all but shouted. "I was looking for you. I'm, like, so excited that we've got a chance to do extra credit for this class," I gushed. "Believe me, I need it."

He smiled at me sympathetically. It was all the encouragement I needed.

"But *you* really seem to get the hang of it," I commented. "So maybe you've got some time, like, this weekend, to go over it with me?"

He shrugged. "Sure, why not?"

It wasn't the most gracious response I'd ever gotten, but there was no need to quibble. "So, um, it's Wednesday. How about tomorrow, maybe around six?"

He frowned. "I don't think I can make it then."

I nodded and went for broke. "Right. Duh. Thursday, whole start of the weekend and everything. I'm sure your girlfriend would be thrilled if you told her you were busy *studying.*"

He looked at me for a moment, then burst out laughing. "Yeah," he said. "Well, no. I mean, I don't have a girlfriend."

Had I really read him so wrong?

"But I've got tickets to this gallery showing downtown that starts at seven. And my boyfriend would be really pissed if I missed it."

Yes, yes, I *had* really read him so wrong.

Anyway, I think we're going to meet up on Saturday. Which is actually good news because I think I need to pass comp sci more than I need to find a date. Though, of course, it would have been great to kill two birds with one stone.

—xx

9/28, 3:34 p.m.
from: kissandtellen@shemail.net
to: cbclarkson@woodmanuniv.edu
re: uh-oh

Oh, my. Should I be concerned about this little comp sci grade situation? Don't believe a word of it, kid—you'll never need this stuff in "real life." Now, the motifs of the female anatomy found in third-world feminist literature? Yeah, that's the stuff of six-figure salaries.

Do the extra credit and I won't say anything to Mom and Dad.

And re: your unreliable gay-dar? Shame on you! Surely I've taught you better than that!

9/30, 6:56 p.m.
from: kissandtellen@shemail.net
to: cbclarkson@woodmanuniv.edu
re: hello?

Haven't heard from you in two days. Slightly concerned. Was only kidding about the comp sci grade, you know. You'll just have to do extra well in women's history to compensate. Which is as it should be, anyway.

Please shoot at least a quick note to reassure me that you haven't been dragged off, *Mr. Goodbar*–style, by your most recent target? Okay? Because then I really *would* have to tell Mom and Dad.

10/1/04, 8:53 p.m.
from: cbclarkson@woodmanuniv.edu
to: clnorton@woodmanuniv.edu,
kissandtellen@shemail.net
re: Sorry . . .

. . . to have been so MIA. Apparently raising one's average from an F to a sweet D– requires some serious mental energy. Not a lot left over for writing.

Lest you think that I'd forgotten, "target practice" is proceeding with its typical semi-smooth regularity. To recap:

•**Tuesday, 9/27:** Delivery boy at the *Chronicle* office. Dropping off some paper goods. I mentioned that his uniform really brought out the . . . yellow in his eyes. He looked at me as though he'd won the lottery. I guess he doesn't get that a lot.

•**Wednesday, 9/28:** Jesse in comp sci. We've been down that road already. Let's not go there again.

•**Thursday, 9/29:** Neo-beatnik I met at on-campus poetry slam. (Our friend Shelley had entered a poem, and Charlie and I went in support.) The look: black-on-black clothing, goatee, John Lennon glasses. All was a-okay until he asserted that I was "altering his experience of reality," at which point I decided I needed to find a new reality of my own.

Besides, I don't even *own* a black ribbed turtleneck.

•**Friday, 9/30:** Cool skate-punker with shiny streaks of blue through his hair. Very counter-culture. I was pretty impressed with myself. Charlie and I picked him up with a friend in Porter Square, at Gabe's favorite CD shop. But we had to put them back down again when I caught my "target" lifting lens cleaners and stuffing them down his pants. Highly problematic scenario on a number of levels.

•**Saturday, 10/1:** "Target #28(!) was a sweet-looking redhead—a first for me!—at the Red Sky café in the heart of our little town center. We were each waiting for our designer drinks by the coffee bar when I struck up a bit of conversation. To my delight, he bit. Alas, I knew we were not meant to be when, as our coffees arrived, he took a sip of double-iced-latte, grimaced, and screamed to the barista, "Are you SURE this is skim?" He shoved his drink back down on the counter, sloshing potentially fattening coffee goo everywhere, and stormed out. Which was just fine by me. Coffee-rage: highly unattractive.

Of course, each of these encounters is a learning experience, blah, blah, blah . . . And I almost can't believe that I only have two left. Almost. But then I think back to some of the more dismal highlights of the experience and it all becomes incredibly vivid again. Sunday, and Monday, and then it's back to the life of a regular old single girl, for better or for worse.

Haven't heard from Drew since he went back. Which is, of course, as we had decided. But still unsettling.

Anyway, can't dwell. T minus forty-eight hours and counting until the extra credit is due. And I *need* credit where credit is due.

Hardy har har.

—xx

10/2, 9:07 p.m.
from: cbclarkson@woodmanuniv.edu
to: kissandtellen@shemail.net,
clnorton@woodmanuniv.edu
re: I have . . .

. . . some news.

You might want to sit down for this one.

Now, I know that as of yesterday I was up to #28 on my "target practice," and that it seemed as though I was careening toward finishing the game much in the same position that I had begun it—that is to say, single. Oh sure, skills, new friends, yadda yadda— reasons abound as to why the game could never be considered a total waste. But as I was saying ever so recently, the fact remained that the game was almost over and, for what it was worth, I was still single. Cord-less, and single. And that was sort of an anticlimax to all of this flirt, flirt, flirting going on right and left, no?

NO?

No.

I had planned to meet up with Gabe on Sunday to go over his pop culture paper outline. Other than a quick e-mail of my

Mad Salad article, and a brief conversation of the when/where of our study session, we really hadn't spoken at all this week. Not even in class. But I was busy—what with the failing of the comp sci, the heavy therapy sessions for Charlie re: her evil pledge stepsister, and, you know, "target practice." Way too busy to dwell.

Sunday rolled around and I was ready; detached, focused, and fully prepared to concentrate on Gabe's outline rather than his latest iron-on T-shirt logo, or the finer points of his last column.

Charlie had bribed me, paradoxically, with chocolate, to hit the gym with her again, and I did, spending a cool forty-five minutes safely spinning away on a stationary bike. I came home, showered, and threw on my "weekend casual" outfit: my best jeans, and a hoodie in the perfect shade of plum.

I confess, there may have been some blow-drying involved.

Okay, it's possible I wasn't as detached as I'm making it out.

But, hey—I decided it's okay to want to put

my best foot forward. I mean, you never know when you're going to happen upon your next target.

And how!

We were set to meet at 2:00. I arrived at 1:43. Yes, friends—1:43 was the precise moment that the life of one Claudia Beth Clarkson took a turn for the unexpected.

Having seventeen minutes to spare, I stopped off in the computer lab to check my e-mail. I sidled up to an empty terminal and grabbed at the mouse, clicking away. It only took a second to realize that my screen was completely dark. Totally out of service. I looked up to see that literally every other terminal in the room was taken. Annoying.

Damn.

"Yeah, that one's not working."

I hadn't even realized I'd spoken out loud until my neighbor at the next terminal responded to my little temper tantrum. He didn't sound at all fazed. If anything, he sounded mildly amused. This was, of course, even more annoying to me.

"Such a pain," I said, dangerously on

the verge of a full-on rant. "How long are you going to—"

I turned to confront my neighbor and froze.
My neighbor was adorable.

He stood about five feet ten inches and had a nice build. He wore a rumpled button-down over a T-shirt, but even through the layers I could tell that he was fit but not a crazed bodybuilder type. He wore lose cords, and scuffed trail shoes that suggested actual trail use. His eyes were the color of my best jeans (post–coffee stain removal, of course), and his hair was sandy and tousled, about a week or two away from needing a trim.

I was gone.

"I'm done, if you need this," he offered, eyes twinkling.

"Oh, uh—that's really nice of you," I said awkwardly.

He logged off and stepped away from his computer so I could slide myself in. But he didn't walk away. Instead, he stood there, watching me, that same bemused grin playing steadily on his lips.

I didn't mind.

"So you knew that terminal wasn't working?" I asked, glancing at him from the corner of my eye while at the same time sifting through my e-mail in-box.

"Guilty as charged," he said, putting his hands up in a "busted" gesture.

"Nice," I teased. "Very chivalrous."

His smile stretched wider. "I had my reasons."

"Oh?"

"Well, it was the perfect opportunity to start a conversation with you."

Oh.

And that was it. I closed out my in-box without even checking the remainder of my messages. He walked me upstairs into the front pavilion, where we sank into the large armchairs and exchanged the superficialities. He's a junior, he lives uphill, in Rigby Hall. He interns as a photography assistant at the *Boston Beacon,* a paper that operates out of the financial district. He's a double-major: finance and international relations. He loves sushi. He saw me in the Brew and Gold a week ago, didn't get it together in time to approach me before I left, and has been wandering the campus on high alert, waiting to see me again. He promised himself he wouldn't let another opportunity go wasted.

And, of course, he didn't.

We're going for sushi tomorrow night.

His name is Sean. Sean Brightman.

Mrs. Sean Brightman . . .

Needless to say, I was ten minutes late meeting with Gabe. Which is totally unprecedented behavior. But I'm done with my unrequited Gabe-crush, done with "target practice," done with doubting my feminine wiles.

Starting now.

—xx

Ten

When two binary code sequences are merged into an algorithmic pattern, the resulting program will be run at a . . .

mrs. Sean Brightman
Claudia Brightman
Claudia and Sean Brightman
Sean and Claudia Brightman
mr. and mrs. Brightman

The "consciousness raising" groups of the early 1970s were considered a harbinger to the new feminist era in which "politicizing

the personal" was the order of
the . . .

It is with great pleasure that
Sean Matthew Brightman and
Claudia Beth Clarkson invite
you to join them on June 14,
20__, as they are joined in
holy . . .

The responsibility of newscasters
to censor the violent content of
their broadcast during prime-time
hours has long been . . .

CBB

CBB

CBB

I shoved aside the piles of reading that
had been gathering dust since I'd sat down
at my desk. It was useless; my eyes danced
across the page, unprocessing regardless of
subject matter. I was utterly and completely consumed with Sean.

It was wonderful.

It had been a week since we'd met and, in that time, we'd spent some part of every day—not to mention every night—together. Sean was friendly, outgoing, giving, and uncomplicated. I adored spending time with him. He was smart, and always made me laugh. In all my days (twenty-eight, to be exact) of "target practice," it had never occurred to me that the game could ever lead somewhere. Certainly not to a new maybe-boyfriend.

Because that's what Sean was shaping up to be. I didn't want to jump the gun, or assume too much too soon, but the truth of the matter was that I was head over heels for him. Around Sean, all of the insanity and uncertainty of being on my own for the first time melted away. With him, I felt comfortable, stable, safe, and warm.

mrs. Sean Brightman

I could only guess what sort of impact he'd have on my GPA—we hadn't gotten our extra-credit scores back from Hartridge yet, but at the moment, I couldn't have cared less.

The door burst open and Charlie flounced in, dropping dramatically onto her bed. She groaned, leaned back against her pillows, and flung an arm over her eyes as though the light was killing her. I didn't bother to point out that it was seven thirty at night and the only glow in the room was coming from my tiny desk lamp. She'd been doing this more and more over the course of the week—coming home, dropping dramatically onto her bed, and groaning, usually due to Anu-related issues. How could I not sympathize? I felt partially responsible for the situation, and it sounded like Anu was really being horrible.

I swiveled around in my chair so that I was facing her, even though she still had one arm over her eye and really wouldn't have known, either way. "Tell."

Charlie sighed. "Today, we had to show our pledge books to the pledge master," she explained. Their pledge books reflected their "scores" in the pledging process, chronicling signatures of sisters interviewed, tasks completed, pranks, boys, the letters of the Greek alphabet . . . it never ended. The amount of useless information contained in those pledge books was staggering. Charlie's grades were fine—more than fine, really (one of the tenets of the Georgia Peach mantle involved scholarship, as a matter of fact), but I figured if it weren't for the energy going into her pledging, the girl would be a national merit scholar. Or at least dean's list.

I had an idea, however, that her pledge book was probably not in the shape that it needed to be in, all things considered.

"Let me guess—there's a problem with yours?"

She sat up on her bed and pulled her hair into a ponytail secured at the nape of her neck. "Well, for starters, I don't have enough signatures."

"Charlie, how is that possible? I know for a fact that you had lunch with at least six of the upperclassmen last week."

"Exactly. And normally a big sister would let me count all six. But, according to Anu, the whole point of the signature is to indicate that I had an up-close-and-personal interaction with a sister. Therefore, there's no way that this could take place at a lunch with four other girls. Which means that *all* of the signatures from that lunch are null and void. And I'm at least ten signatures behind."

"That sucks," I said, clucking my tongue sympathetically.

"The worst thing about it is that, technically, she's right, and so there's not much I can do. Complaining won't get me anywhere—and I really don't want to complain, anyway. That would only make her hate me more."

"Smart thinking," I agreed.

"And get this," she continued, warming to her story. "All of the pledges have to paint the cannon, right?"

The cannon was a landmark situated just in front of the president's house, at the top of the hill. It's been around since Woodman was first established. No one knew what it signified. These days, the thing to do was to paint it: team colors the night before homecoming, pledge colors the night before initiation, for your best friend on her birthday, as a declaration of love . . . you get the picture. The catch was that the cannon could only be painted at night, and on any given night, so many different groups were vying for the chance to work a little Michelangelo that, if you wanted to ensure that your artwork made it to daybreak, you were basically up all night, guarding it. I could see how the activity could foster school spirit, team unity, etc., etc., but to me it just seemed like prime sleeping hours gone to waste.

"Yeah?"

"Well, we were divided into groups and assigned different nights, you know— based on our class schedules and who was available what night. Trick was that we were all going to be doing it in groups. But, of course, guess which one of us is groupless?"

"I'm guessing you."

"You're guessing right. Me! Painting the cannon—and then guarding the cannon. All by myself. All night long. Lousy, right?"

"Definitely lousy," I agreed. "Did you say anything when you found out?"

"Believe it or not, I did. I mean, you know the last thing that I want to do is rock the boat, but I couldn't not say something.

So I just *casually* asked Anu how it was that the schedules worked out the way they did. You know, in that I was the *only* one able to paint tonight. Which of course set her off into a twenty-minute conniption about whether or not my dedication was up to the level befitting a Tri-Delt. And then I had to backtrack like crazy."

"Oh, Charlie, I'm sorry," I said. "When are you painting?"

"Tonight," she said. "Midnight." She brightened momentarily. "Want to go with me to town to pick up paint?"

I winced. "I can't," I said. "I'm meeting Sean in half an hour. We were going to see that new James Bond movie."

"Don't you hate James Bond?" she pointed out.

"'Hate' is a strong word, Charlie," I admonished. "I think 'vehemently dislike' is the more accurate term."

"Then why would you go to see it?" she asked.

"Because Sean likes it. And I like Sean," I said. "And he promised to go see that new Julia Roberts thing with me next week in exchange."

"*I* would have gone to see the Julia Roberts thing with you next week," she said.

"I know," I agreed. "But he has nicer shoulders than you do."

"That is true," she said thoughtfully. She lay back down on her bed again, awash in self-pity. "Fine, then. Go see your boy movie. Leave the dirty work of pledging to me." She assumed her traditional arm-flung-over-eye posture. "At least one of us should be having fun tonight."

"Oh, don't worry," I teased. "I'll definitely be having enough fun for both of us."

A funny thing, the word "love," don't you think? Overuse and abuse in the pop culture has led to sickly sweet associations with the term: little girls with stars in their eyes, animated cupids following them to and fro, arrows pointed squarely at chests, hearts thump-thumping deep outlines practically out of chests and into the atmosphere (in a cute way, of course). I used to assume that these representations were exaggerated, that love couldn't possibly be as simplistic as sugar and spice and everything nice.

Boy, was I ever wrong.

I suppose this was what it was like when I first met Drew. But, of course, four years is a long time to be with one person. By our senior year there were certain assumptions in place, certain means of taking each other for granted. A point in time, for example, when I stopped wearing lip gloss on our dates. Which of course isn't exactly a crime, but should give you a sense of where we were.

Sean was lip gloss worthy, all the way. I couldn't remember the last time I got so excited about going to see a movie. A movie I didn't even want to see, for that matter. But James Bond took on new life when Sean was sitting next to me, holding my hand. And it wasn't just 007. With Sean around, everything seemed just that much more appealing: from the dreggy remains of my mocha Frappuccino to the unnecessary torture of the elliptical machine at the gym.

I was one smitten kitten.

I melted over his sensitivity; I swooned at the color of his eyes. But it was more than that. I'd never known someone to take such an interest in *me,* so quickly. It turned out that once he found out who I was, he'd gone back and read all of my articles in the *Chronicle* (he was particularly impressed with my knowledge of Latin-punk fusion). He came to the gym with Charlie and me twice this week. He immediately took to Troy, and even made it a point to ask them to double last Thursday when we went for Thai down in Inman Square.

We spent last Saturday at Faneuil Hall, trying on crazy sunglasses (him) and retro-eighties earrings (me). Monday, of course, was the action flick. And when I mentioned to him how badly I felt for Charlie, he insisted that we pick up some hot chocolate and french fries and bring them by the cannon for her. We stood guard with her for about three hours, Sean regaling us with his plans to study in Belize over the spring semester.

I, for one, could just die.

But I won't. I'm meeting Sean for dinner and I don't want to be late.

Thursday, about two weeks after our James Bond outing, Sean and I were set to meet for another on-campus poetry slam. Shelley had submitted a piece again, and, as usual, Charlie and I wanted to show our support.

We hit the local pizza place, Luigi's, beforehand to fuel up. Troy wanted pepperoni, I wanted mushrooms. Sean hit upon the brilliant plan of going half and half.

"Dude, I do *not* understand how you could possibly not like this," Troy said, folding his slice in half and wolfing down half of it in one bite. It left streaks of sauce across his chin, which I didn't bother to point out. He plucked a piece of pepperoni off the remainder of the slice and sucked it down eagerly.

I glanced at his paper plate. The pools of grease that had collected were turning a toxic shade of orange.

"I don't know, Troy, I guess it's just a little too much for me," I said, shrugging. "To each his own."

"To each *her* own," Sean corrected me, hugging me to him.

"True enough, babe," I agreed.

"Do you think that weird mime guy is going to be there tonight?" Charlie asked. "Because I don't know if I can sit through that again without laughing, you know."

"Not sure. They didn't run the lineup in the *Chronicle* this time," I said.

"Oh, duh! I should have checked," Charlie said. "I was too busy reading the personals. You were right, they're really funny."

"What's so funny about personals?" Troy asked. "Is it, like, 'SWM seeks model for long walks on beach'?"

Charlie reached out and dabbed at his chin with her napkin. This was one part cute, one part disturbing. "No, it's this thing Claudia told me about. Like, how you can take personals out for your friends and stuff, on their birthdays and whatever—"

"Oh yeah, I've seen those—," Sean chimed in.

"But the thing is that the *Chronicle* staff do this thing where they bury these messages to one another in the personals. And you never really know when they're going to be in there or what they'll be for. You just have to keep checking, on the off chance that you'll find something interesting."

"Wait—so you saw something?" I asked. I hadn't checked the personals in a few days. The number of days since I'd met Sean, to be precise. "What was it?"

Charlie dug into her bag and produced a beat-up copy of that day's paper. She flipped the pages until they were open to the classifieds:

MIDNIGHT IHOP. COLBY AT 11:30.

It was from O'Shea, I could tell. Just like with the roller disco; he loved quirky outings that fostered team-building.

"You gonna go?" Sean asked.

"Huh? Oh, no." Not only had I not checked the personals in ten days, but I also hadn't requested any new assignments from Gabe, either. Our post-Drew study date had been awkward, and besides that, I'd been busy with my own paper and the extra credit for comp sci. And, of course, busy with Sean. And with Charlie, whose pledge-related freak-outs were growing increasingly common.

So I hadn't read the personals, talked to Gabe, or been down to the paper in over a week. Which was pretty atypical behavior for me. I hadn't exactly missed it, as such, or I suppose I would have gotten it together to get down there. I guessed that the trick to getting over Gabe was falling for someone else. But the ad in front of me was proof positive that life went on without me. The staff had plans for big fun tonight and they didn't involve me. It didn't matter that I was the one who in effect had excluded myself. It still felt wrong.

I pushed away my pizza and took a hearty slurp on my Diet Coke.

"Why not?" Sean pressed. "The slam starts in half an hour. It should be over by ten, tops. You'll have plenty of time to catch a ride, I'm sure."

"I just don't want to," I said, testy. Why did Sean have to be so *understanding* about it all, dammit? It didn't matter that my response to the dumb personals ad was immature and overreactionary. I didn't want solutions; I just wanted to sulk for a little bit without anyone asking questions. But for some reason, Sean, seeing that I was upset, wasn't going to just let it go. No matter how much I wished he would. And why?

Because he was Sean, that's why.

10/17, 6:31 p.m.
from: cbclarkson@woodmanuniv.edu
to: gflynn12@woodmanuniv.edu
re: paper

 Hey—

 I waited for you after class, but you must have

slipped out some secret door or something. I wanted to see what you got on the paper.

And also to ask you—do you have anyone covering the West Hall Halloween party this year? I hear it's one of the best on-campus events of the year. If not, can I put in my bid? It's been a while since I've darkened the doorways of the *Chronicle*.

Did you guys have fun at IHOP?

—xx

10/18, 4:48 p.m.
from: clnorton@woodmanuniv.edu
to: cbclarkson@woodmanuniv.edu
re: fw: appropriate attire—AAARGH
See below.
[note: forwarded message attached]

from: ashah5@woodmanuniv.edu
to: clnorton@woodmanuniv.edu
re: appropriate attire
Charlie—
I couldn't help but notice that you weren't wearing your pledge pin at the gym today. I'm sure you're well aware that the pledge pin is considered a symbol of status

and a means of indicating to the entire extended campus your commitment to the Tri-Delts. If in fact you find it to be too obtrusive, perhaps we can dig up something more . . . subtle for you to wear?

You can pick up your new accessory from the house anytime after four.

10/18, 5:15 p.m.
from: cbclarkson@woodmanuniv.edu
to: clnorton@woodmanuniv.edu
re: re: fw: appropriate attire—AAARGH
I'm almost afraid to ask—what is it?

10/18, 5:54 p.m.
from: clnorton@woodmanuniv.edu
to: cbclarkson@woodmanuniv.edu
re: re: re: fw: appropriate attire—AAARGH
Did you see *The Cat in the Hat*? That crap movie with Mike Myers?

DO YOU REMEMBER HIS HAT?

10/18, 6:34 p.m.
from: cbclarkson@woodmanuniv.edu
to: clnorton@woodmanuniv.edu
re: re: re: re: fw: appropriate attire—AAARGH
Oh. My. God.

10/20, 6:20 p.m.
from: cbclarkson@woodmanuniv.edu
to: gflynn12@woodmanuniv.edu
re: Out of sight, out of mind?

Heya—

I realize I'm walking the fine line between casual acquaintance and stalker, but I figured it was worth one more shot, on the off chance that you were not, in fact, avoiding me, but rather, trapped, somewhere, under a large object.

I noticed you weren't in class yesterday. Where ya been, man? Surely you haven't quit school to follow the Dead. You never struck me as especially granola. . . .

—xx

10/24, 3:17 p.m.
from: gflynn12@woodmanuniv.edu
to: cbclarkson@woodmanuniv.edu
re: re: Out of sight, out of mind?

Not avoiding you. Buried in anthro reading. IHOP was fun, though we missed you. Got a B on the media paper, so thanks for all of your help (and congrats on beating my sorry ass!).

I should be in class today. See you there?

—G

p.s.: about West—not sure about that. Can you talk to Abby Dalton? She handles the on-campus sort of stuff. adalton@woodmanuniv.edu.

p.p.s.: the Dead are over, Claud. Jerry's gone. If I were going to hit the road, it'd be to find the Beastie Boys. I think they're somewhere in Brooklyn.

Suddenly, it was late October, and the West Hall Halloween party was upon us. (Funny how time flies when you're having fun.) Sean and I decided to go as Bonnie and Clyde, and Abby Dalton agreed to let me write up the scene for the *Chronicle.* I'd been away from the paper for way too long.

West was the oldest dorm on campus, and its architecture reflected as much: sweeping, Gothic arches and deep, dark stone moldings. It would have made the perfect haunted house even smack dab in

235

the middle of Easter. The party committee (whom I'd interviewed earlier that day) had spared no expense on decor. Cobwebs hung from every doorway, and atmospheric moans and rattles echoed through the hallways. At eleven, the party was already kicking. Sean and I helped ourselves to some candy corn and stood off to one corner of the common room, happy to observe. I wasn't much for talking. I'd been quiet all day, actually. Nothing was bothering me as such, but I guess . . . I was in a mood.

Sensing my tension, Sean offered to grab us some beers, disappearing into the hallway where the keg was set up.

"Dammit, I chipped a nail."

I looked up and laughed. It was Gabe, done up as a completely punked-out Sid Vicious. His hair stood up in bright white Billy Idol peaks. His nails were painted black, though I could see none of the chips he referenced.

"Where's your partner in crime?" he asked, glancing back and forth as though he half-expected Sean to come swinging into the room on a vine, bat him aside, and carry me off in one fell swoop.

"You mean Sean?" I asked, confused. Why did Gabe know I had a boyfriend? It wasn't a secret, but I hadn't gone out of my way to talk about it with anyone from the paper. Had hardly even been down to the paper lately. And what did Gabe care about gossip, anyway? Weird. "Beer run. He said he'll be right back."

"Well, then, he probably will," Gabe reasoned.

"Yes, he's very reliable," I agreed.

"Lucky you," Gabe said.

Before I could respond to that, I felt a tap on my shoulder. "Look what I found you!"

I looked. Sean stood next to me, palm outstretched. He was cupping a handful of miniature chocolates. My eyes lit up. "Where?"

"In the lobby," he said. "We missed it when we came in. And it's Hershey's, not that second-rate generic brand that you hate. I made sure to double check."

"That's awfully conscientious of you," Gabe said, sniffing.

"Sean, have you met Gabe?" I asked, turning from one to the other like a deranged social coordinator. What the hell was wrong with me? I was introducing a friend to my boyfriend. No big. "Gabe Flynn, Sean Brightman. Gabe is the arts editor—"

"Right, for the *Chronicle*!" Sean finished, excited. "Man, I *love* your column!"

"Yeah, thanks."

Sean threw an arm over my shoulder and gave it a squeeze. "Claudia is always saying how she owes the whole journalism thing to you. That's really cool."

"Well, uh, Claudia's a great writer," Gabe mumbled.

The room felt thick and hot, and Gabe's face was growing red and sweaty. Meanwhile, Sean still had his arm wrapped around me, hugging away happily. Was the punch spiked? I set it down on the table.

"You know," Gabe said, echoing my thoughts, "I think—I'm getting kind of hot."

"Probably the leather," Sean suggested rather pragmatically, pointing at Gabe's pants.

"Yeah, uh, I think I'm gonna get some punch." He ran his fingers through his hair, only to shower himself in the spray-on bleached-blond effect he'd somehow managed.

"But the punch is right here," Sean pointed out mildly.

"Right. I meant some fresh air. That's what I need," Gabe said. He reached to run his fingers through his hair again, then remembered the spray. He dropped his hand to his side awkwardly. "I'll see you in a few?"

"Sure," Sean said, still with the pleasant smile. "We'll be here!"

But we didn't see him again for the rest of the night.

I never did get to the bottom of Gabe's behavior at the party. Maybe he *was* suffering from heat exhaustion. Who knew? I mean, the kid was working part-time in addition to his responsibilities at the paper. Not to mention his actual classes. I had no idea what courses he was taking other than pop culture, or how he was doing in them. Or maybe he had some form of low-level bipolar disorder. I mean, how well did I really know him, after all?

Not very. Not very well at all. And meanwhile, a month into our relationship and Sean and I were still going strong. Just yesterday he had used the *B* word for the very first time. As in:

"No, let me get this."

"Why, Sean, you shouldn't—"

"Claudia, will you let your boyfriend pay for your fries, please?"

Which was, of course, enough to shut me up.

The other thing I never got to the bottom of was my strange mood on the night of the West Hall Halloween party. But I decided to chalk it up to free-floating PMS or something. I mean, everything was cool with Sean. Charlie and Ellen both approved. I was writing for the paper, I was passing comp sci, and all in all, life was good.

So why was I so hung up on Gabe's personality issue?

I wasn't, I decided. I wasn't at all. I was 120 percent over Gabe—had been since the night at the roller disco. Had been since "target practice" began. Sean was the one.

But there was something I hadn't told anyone. Something so insignificant that I couldn't imagine telling anyone; it almost didn't even bear mentioning. Silly, even. I had no idea why I was still thinking about it.

See, Sunday night, the night after the West Hall Halloween party, had been my one-month anniversary with Sean. And I was pleased to discover that, on the subject of anniversaries, he was almost as much of a girly-girl as I was. He insisted that we return to the site of our first date: the sushi restaurant he loved over in the theater district. It was perfect. We took a private booth, kicked our shoes off, and cozied up, playing footsie inside the well. We shared edamame and drank sake like it was going out of style. There were toasts aplenty, to first semesters, to first encounters, to lost Internet connections. . . .

Where was the bad?

After dinner, Sean walked me home. I had an early meeting with a study group on Sunday, but I promised him I'd come by as soon as it was over. He was totally understanding and didn't pressure me at all to come back to his dorm. We stood outside of the front door to my dorm, arms circling each other's waists.

"Thanks so much for tonight," I said.

"Anytime," he said. "And I hope there will be lots of other times in our future. Anniversary times," he said, reaching out and smoothing an errant strand of hair from my face.

"Me too," I agreed, sighing happily. "I'm sorry I have to cut our night short."

"Not a problem, sweetie. You'll just have to come by first thing tomorrow when you're done studying."

"Of course, I said I would. We're meeting so early, you'll definitely still be in bed by the time I'm done. I'll bring coffee and bagels."

He took my face in both hands. "I can't wait." He leaned forward and kissed me on the forehead. "Be good, Bee," he said.

And then he left.

It was a cute moment. Sweet, even. Endearing. What with the forehead kiss and all. And yet, for some reason, that tiny, insignificant phrase left me with a nagging feeling in the pit of my stomach. I couldn't figure out why. So there were two things on my mind: my boyfriend's term of endearment, and Gabe's abrupt shift in personality. Neither one really should have caused me so much angst. But they both did. Were still. And I couldn't put my finger on why.

The whole thing was driving me crazy.

Eleven

By Thursday I wasn't feeling any better. In fact, the small nagging feeling gnawing at the lining of my stomach had progressed to a full-blown preoccupation that was interfering with just about all of my basic day-to-day tasks. That morning, I had e-mailed my bio assignment to my history professor, and vice versa, and had nearly brushed my teeth with Charlie's hair gel that night. When I finally climbed into bed, I lay, eyes wide open, contemplating the ceiling for what felt like hours.

"Be good, Bee."

Sean had said that, and had kissed me on the forehead, every time we'd parted company since Saturday. And for some reason it was grating on me like nails on a chalkboard. Meanwhile, Gabe and I were studiously avoiding each other in pop culture, and I hadn't been down to the paper once since turning in the West Hall piece.

I glanced at the clock: 1:02. Great. I could only imagine how much fun my morning classes were going to be. But sleep wasn't coming anytime soon, so there was no point in lying in bed. I hauled myself up and padded over to my computer. Fortunately, Charlie was out on some Anu-related errand, so I didn't have to worry about disturbing her. I opened my e-mail in-box and began sifting through and cleaning it out. The task felt tidy and productive, a means of sorting out my emotional clutter as much as anything else.

I hadn't done an e-mail purge since school had started nearly two months ago. I don't know what I'd been expecting to find. I skimmed through e-mails from Ellen bitching about Daria's mood swings and the need for better organic produce down at Bryn Mawr. I noticed with some guilt that I hadn't written to my parents nearly as often as I'd meant to.

And suddenly, there it was, in big block letters. And old e-mail from Drew. His first to me at school. Seeing Drew's name and address pop up on my screen hit me like a sucker punch. I was winded. Knowing full well that this verged on Very Bad Idea territory, I opened up the e-mail.

Hi, Bee—
All moved in. Completely exhausted. Wondering if consuming the contents of an entire six-pack of beer on my own was such a fabulous idea.

Never a good idea. I was now in a position to speak authoritatively on the subject.

College! Crazy, right? I can hardly believe four years have passed since we first met. I know I've said it before, but I am so thankful that you found me and, uh, *encouraged* (let's be honest here—forced) me to join the newspaper. And then, you know, *encouraged* me to ask you out.

I'm feeling a little nostalgic, my dear.

Bee good, Bee (hardy har har) and have an excellent first day. Keep in touch, but don't feel like you *have* to write me back ASAP. I get the independence thing.

He was right; even sober, the nostalgia factor was high. But that wasn't what struck me. I paused, and reread the last paragraph:

"Bee good, Bee."

The same exact phrase that Sean had taken to uttering every time we parted company.

Eerie coincidence? Not necessarily. I could tick off at least five friends and acquaintances who had at some point bastardized my middle initial into some permutation of "Bee" as a nickname. But there was something about the fact that Sean's pet name for me paralleled Drew's pet name for me, something deeply unnerving. Obviously, I could talk to Sean. I could let him know that when he called me "Bee" it dredged up weird associations. I was sure he wouldn't be offended, and that he'd have no problem finding me another sickeningly sweet nickname. But with a sinking feeling, I began to mentally catalog the various other ways in which Drew and Sean overlapped. I couldn't help myself. And, unfortunately, it was easy to come up with a bunch of examples.

Both were cute in a very accessible, meet-the-parents sort of way; not too jock-y, not too alt-y, not too nerdy. Both were disarmingly friendly and warm. Both were considerate almost to a fault, if there was such a thing.

Both were comfortable.

But hadn't I broken up with Drew to break *out* of my comfort zone?

By the fourth year with Drew we were pretty much operating on autopilot. The butterflies were gone. And while I suppose in any relationship the initial passion eventually dies down, I'd hope that it wouldn't have to disappear completely. Halfway through senior year, seeing Drew walk into a classroom just wasn't sending my heart rate into high gear anymore, and that was how I knew: After four years, we were done.

Was the same true of me and Sean after only four weeks?

I gazed over the screen of my laptop and out the window, pensive. The fact of the matter was that while I adored spending time with Sean, physical contact with him was pleasant rather than over-the-top, out-of-control electric. In other words, a lot like the warm, familiar, friendly sex I had with Drew. And the things I liked best about Sean's personality were the things I'd always loved about Drew. Not to mention, we spent time doing a lot of the same things that Drew and I had done when we were together.

Had I, in my weakened and vulnerable state as suddenly single (not to mention, a freshman), gone and cloned my last relationship?

I didn't want to think so. Because if that was true, then where were Sean and I headed? But the fact of the matter was that when Sean walked into the room, I experienced a pleasant buzz. That wasn't love, I knew. That wasn't even excitement. Excitement was feeling like you were going to explode out of your skin just from standing next to someone for a fraction of a second.

It was the feeling I got when Gabe was around.

I knew Gabe was a lost cause. He'd

been awkward and moody with me basically since the day we'd met. And besides, his girlfriend was a bona fide goddess. It was actually her nickname, for chrissake. There was no competing with that. But whether or not Gabe was available, I couldn't keep lying to myself. I couldn't pretend that Sean and I were falling in love. I owed him honesty.

And I owed myself even more.

The door burst open, and Charlie swept in. She stopped, sensing my mood. "What's going on?"

"I have to go to class," I told her, standing up and gathering my bag, wallet, and keys. "But, I just . . ." I sighed. "I think I have to break up with Sean."

11/4, 10:14 a.m.
from: cbclarkson@woodmanuniv.edu
to: kissandtellen@shemail.net
re: breaking news

I think I have to break up with Sean.

No, I *know* I have to break up with Sean.

I know I told you that he was wonderful and that I adored him. This is still true. But another truism is that I'm afraid I got involved for the wrong reasons: comfort, familiarity, stability. All great things, but they need to go hand in hand with honest-to-goodness passion, don't you think?

Well, I do.

And, unfortunately, being around Sean just doesn't make me dizzy in the same way that being around Gabe does.

Gabe may be off-limits, I know, but the thing is that just knowing that I have the capacity to feel the way I do about him makes me reluctant to settle for feeling anything less. I deserve to feel dizzy (well, you know what I mean). And Sean deserves someone who feels dizzy about him.

So that's that. We're supposed to meet up for coffee after class. I guess I'll tell him then.

Wish me luck.

—xx

11/4, 11:56 a.m.
from: kissandtellen@shemail.net
to: cbclarkson@woodmanuniv.edu
re: Sadness!

Claud, my heart is breaking for you! I'm sorry that it's not going to work out for you and Sean, but it sounds like you've really thought things through and that it's for the best. I think it's very brave of you to hold out for the real deal, and I just know that, in the long run, you'll find someone who will make you so dizzy, you're practically sick to your stomach (in a good way).

I met Sean outside of Brew and Gold after my comp sci lab. I could tell he'd just woken up. He had that sleep-confused look on his face, and his hair was half-brushed. It was pretty cute, and made my job just that much more difficult. After we bought our coffees, he gestured to one of the couches, but I suggested instead that we walk over to the library roof. It was a clear, crisp day and I thought the view would be nice.

We trudged up Memorial Steps and past the academic quad, down toward the library. I couldn't help but notice that Sean hadn't bothered to try to hold my hand. I wondered if he could sense that something was up.

As we settled ourselves against the railing of the roof, my question was answered. "So," he began, setting his coffee cup down. "What's on your mind?"

I blushed. "How can you tell?"

"Claudia, you haven't said one word since we met at the coffeehouse. For you, that's totally out of character."

"Not true," I protested.

"When have you *ever* gone more than five minutes without speaking?" he teased.

I glared at him, but couldn't really argue. He was right.

"So, spill it," he prompted. "It can't be that bad."

"No, not that bad," I began carefully. "But yeah, there's something."

I tilted my body so that I was facing him more directly. "I really, really like you, Sean."

"But . . ."

"But . . . when I first came to college I made it a point to break up with my long-term boyfriend so that I could stand on my own two feet for a while. Of course, when I got here, and the classes were hard, and the boys were predatory, and the beer was cheap . . . well, suddenly that seemed a lot scarier to me than I had anticipated. And I thought I had lost my touch with guys."

"You? No way."

"Way. *Seriously.* Way. So I practiced going

up to guys and talking, and sometimes it backfired really badly and sometimes it didn't, but for the most part it was what it was. And then, finally, I met you. And it just felt so comfortable, right from the start, and such a relief from trying so hard all the time."

"Okay, Claud, so where's the part where this is a bad thing?"

I smiled sadly. "I guess there isn't one, really. I mean, it's not bad that I met you—it's amazing. But I'm afraid that I'm allowing myself to fall into another situation because it feels comfortable."

"And that's not what you want right now," he finished for me.

I shook my head. "No, it's not."

He sighed deeply. "Well, this isn't what I want, Claud, but I do think it takes guts to choose to be on your own rather than fall back on a relationship."

"Thank you," I said. "I wish you weren't making this so easy for me. It almost makes this all harder."

"Would you rather I tossed my coffee in your face and stormed off?" he said, picking up his cup and pantomiming.

I pretended to consider this for a moment. "It's an idea . . . ," I said. "But no thanks."

He laughed and leaned over to hug me. "I'm not going to sit around waiting for you, obviously," he said. "And, you know, I'm going abroad next semester, anyway, so maybe this is good timing. But if you change your mind or want to just talk, you know where to find me."

"I will," I promised him.

He stood up, zipped his jacket up more tightly and, with a wave, he was gone.

Miraculously, Charlie had a few hours off from pledging hell, and we'd arranged to meet for dinner at Luigi's for pizza. I arrived at seven and settled into a booth. Charlie showed up ten minutes later, looking frazzled. Frazzled was not a look I was accustomed to seeing on Charlie, and it took me a moment to adjust to the wisps of hair escaping from her ponytail in every direction, her untucked shirt, and her shiny T-zone.

"Ugh, I *swear* I am going to kill that girl in her sleep," Charlie groaned, sliding into the seat across from me.

"Anu?" I guessed.

"Yu-huh. Today she wanted me to write a haiku in tribute to one of the Sigma-Nu boys. Then I had to read it as I performed an interpretive dance. All this in front of the Inter-Greek Council at their weekly meeting."

"No!" I gasped. Even for Anu, even for sorority pranks, that sounded bad. A thought occurred to me. "Wait a minute," I said suspiciously. "Which guy?"

"Zach Masters, of course."

"Oh, is she still giving you trouble about him? Doesn't she realize that *I* was the one who was hitting on him?"

"Actually, Claudia, *he* was the one who was hitting on *you*."

"Whatever. Charlie, I think you need to stand up to Anu."

Charlie leaned forward across the table. "Yeah, that's a fabulous idea. Because I never actually *wanted* to be initiated, anyway."

"I'm serious, Charlie. This chick has absolutely no reason to be carrying a vendetta against you, and I think, objectively speaking, that it's pretty obvious she is treating you unfairly in comparison with the other pledges. You need to deal with this. Until you stand up for yourself, she's not going to respect you."

Charlie eyed me for a moment, contemplating.

"You were nervous," I prodded. "The whole Greek scene was new, and it was something you really wanted to be a part of. You didn't want to blow it. But it's *not* like you, and you can't go on like this. Besides, Miss Georgia Peach—didn't you take first in the interview sections of all of your many pageants? If *anyone* can broach a difficult topic diplomatically, it's you."

"You're right!" she said, banging her fist on the table. A few nearby patrons turned to stare. "You're right," she said more quietly, patting the table softly. "I'll call her tonight and ask if we can find a time to sit down and talk. And if she refuses . . ."

"She won't refuse," I said with certainty. "Not if you phrase it in just the right way."

She nodded. "You're right. Have I mentioned that you're right? When did you get so smart?" She leaned across the table and eyed me. "When did you get so *depressed*? What's wrong? Is something wrong? And here I've been blabbing on all about my boring problems."

"No! Well, yes, but I mean, I wanted to hear about your day. I'm glad you're going to talk to Anu. I think it's the only solution."

"Yes, but now we're talking about Claudia," she insisted.

"Well, on the subject of being true to oneself . . . I broke up with Sean today," I confessed.

She made a face. "At least you've got it done with?" she asked uncertainly. "It must be slightly better than having the whole thing hanging over your head?" She sighed heavily. "I just feel like the least perceptive friend in the whole world. Here I thought you guys were so happy."

"We *were* happy," I said. "But, unfortunately, it was more the 'hangin' with your best bud' kind of happy."

"As opposed to the 'rip my clothes off and have your way with me now' kind of happy?" Charlie countered.

"Exactly. And I know that, in a relationship, the stable friendship is as important as the heaving passion, but isn't it okay to want a little bit of both?"

"More than okay," Charlie asserted.

"Anyway, I felt like I was just replicating my relationship with Gabe all over again, and that's the last thing I wanted."

Charlie blinked, but didn't say anything. I was surprised; I'd been expecting something along the lines of a "you go, girl!" or the like. Not the fish-eye she was leveling at me with unnerving intensity.

"Now's the part in the conversation where it's your turn to talk, Charlie," I said, prompting her.

"Claudia, did you hear yourself?" she asked.

"Yeah." I shrugged. "I was replicating my relationship with—" I stopped, color flooding my cheeks. "Yikes."

"Can you tell him how you feel?" she asked. "In the interest of being true to yourself?"

I shook my head vehemently. "Charlie, he has a girlfriend. I'm not a home-wrecker. Or, dorm-wrecker."

"I understand," she said. "I don't like it,

but I understand. I'll talk to Anu tonight. I'll be true enough for the both of us."

I sighed. "It's a deal."

After dinner I headed toward the *Chronicle* office. I wanted to pick up some press releases that I knew were waiting for me. First I swung by the Brew and Gold for a caffeine hit.

"Looking for Gabe?"

It was Kyra, stirring a sprinkle of cinnamon into her soy chai. Even her beverages were serene and elegant.

"Uh, no. I mean, yeah. Well, I was just going to pick up some papers that I need for my next article," I said. "Have you seen him?"

"He went home a few hours ago."

"Oh, cool," I said. I turned to go.

"What's wrong?" she asked.

I paused. Kyra and I weren't exactly best buds. Should I really be confiding in her?

I decided I didn't have anything to lose. "I just broke up with my boyfriend."

Kyra's eyes widened in sympathy. "Oh, I'm sorry. Breaking up sucks."

"Yup," I said shortly.

"I thought . . ." She paused as though she was considering her words. "I thought you were into this dating thing. Gabe told me he heard you talking to your ex-boyfriend at the Tin Room about some quest to meet a certain number of boys."

My cheeks flamed red. "Uh, yeah," I said, mortified. "It was just a joke. A way to get comfortable talking to guys again now that I'm single. Or *was* single. Or am single again."

"I love that idea," she said. "It takes serious balls." I never thought I'd hear someone as delicate as Kyra say the word "balls." I smiled.

Kyra leveled me with a look. "But maybe this is a good thing."

"Meaning?"

"Maybe now you can be with the person you're really crushing on?"

If I thought my cheeks were hot before, my entire face was on fire now. "What do you mean?" I protested weakly.

"Please," Kyra said, smiling. She gathered all of her hair together and secured it into a messy bun. "'Dear Answer Goddess:

I've got a mad crush on this kid at the paper. I think we're friends, but I have no idea whether or not he thinks about me "that way." And I'm afraid to ask, in case he doesn't. What do I do?'"

I froze, mortified. Was I that transparent?

She laughed. "No, you're not that obvious," she said, reading my mind and again suggesting otherwise. "But I'd have to be a moron not to see the chemistry between you and Gabe."

"But—," I stammered, "he's *your* boyfriend. I would *never*—"

"Listen," Kyra said, cutting me off and dropping her voice. "I actually have a secret of my own for you. Since we're being so honest with each other."

I looked at her questioningly.

"Gabe and I are old family friends. We grew up together in Highland Park. Our mothers met while we were in playgroup. He's like a brother to me."

"So you're not together?" I asked, stunned. I thought back to all of the times I'd seen them together, all of the times Kyra had slung an arm around his shoulder or ruffled his hair. I felt like I had at the end of watching *The Sixth Sense:* I'd been hood-winked. Each incident had been a sham; I'd seen what I'd wanted to see, even though, technically, I could now understand that perhaps I'd misinterpreted the situation. Or even been deliberately misled. My eyes narrowed. "But, I thought . . ."

"I know you did," she said. "I think that was a little bit on purpose."

"Do you, um, *like* Gabe?" I asked nervously. Even if they weren't properly together, I wasn't keen on the idea of her as my competition. What with her being a goddess, and all.

"I *love* Gabe," she said. "And, yeah, I guess there's a little part of me that 'likes him likes him.' I could tell that he has feelings for you, and it bothered me. I'm only human, you know. I guess I just sort of wanted to confuse you."

"Well, it worked."

"I know. I'm sorry. Like I said, there was the jealousy factor. There will always be a little part of me that will wonder what it would be like to date Gabe. And then there's the big-sister thing too—I wanted to be sure that you were good enough for him."

I bristled. "And I'm not?" I asked, sitting up straighter in my chair.

"Claudia, when you got here, you were on the rebound. I didn't want Gabe to get hurt." She softened. "He's really into you."

"You're kidding, right?" I asked, barely breathing.

"Think about how he was at that party. He was pissy that you were with Sean. *Were* with Sean. Claudia—you have to tell him. How you feel. How you're *single*. Seriously. I've never seen him look at *anyone* the way he looks at you. And, by the way—"

"Yeah?"

"He *never* gives out passes to shows he wants to see. Let that be a lesson to you."

"I . . . wow." I stood up and stretched. Kyra had dropped a lot on me, all at once. I wasn't sure what to do with it. Talk to Gabe, I supposed, but there was too much going on in my head. I needed to think. I needed some time to myself.

"You need some time to yourself, to think," Kyra said matter-of-factly. "You'll process this tonight and you'll talk to

Gabe this weekend. It'll all be good."

I turned to her. "It's very creepy, the way that you do that," I said.

She smirked. "It's a gift."

I stood and said good-bye. The wheels in my mind were spinning, and I had no idea how to make them stop.

11/7, 8:03 p.m.
from: cbclarkson@woodmanuniv.edu
to: gflynn12@woodmanuniv.edu
re: the midterm

Hey, there—
Wanna be my study buddy?

—xx

On Monday, our professor announced our upcoming pop culture midterm. Monday night, I e-mailed Gabe about studying. I figured a one-on-one session would be a prime opportunity to talk to him about my feelings. And if I chickened out . . . well, at least I would have gotten some studying out of the way.

On Tuesday, I hadn't heard back from him. I decided not to freak about it. Again,

I had no idea what else he had on his plate. So Kyra thought he was interested in me. What did she know? By her own admission, she'd been totally manipulating me for the past two months. I had no concrete proof he'd even given me a second thought since last week at the paper.

On Wednesday, he still hadn't written. By now I was slightly suspicious, more so when he arrived at class late and parked himself directly in the front row, miles from where I was sitting, and defiantly refused any eye contact whatsoever.

I pounced on him the minute that class ended. "Hey," I said, trying desperately to catch my breath and not appear as though I'd streaked down four rows to grab him before he left. "Did you, uh, get my e-mail?"

"Yeah," he said quickly, not meeting my gaze.

"Oh," I said. I paused for a beat. "Um, why didn't you write me back?" I hated the way I sounded: insecure, whiny. Sad.

"I just assumed you were too busy to study," he said evasively.

"Huh?" I said, genuinely puzzled. "Why

would I have asked you to study if I didn't have time?"

"I don't know," he said, still averting his eyes. "Maybe you'd be caught up in something. Or someone else. Like a target."

Now he looked at me. Gone was his usual sunny smile. Instead, he looked confused and a little bit insecure.

"You knew about that," I reminded him. "It was just a dumb game. You heard me talking about it at the Tin Room."

"I thought it was just a way to meet new people," he said. "Until I came by the Brew and Gold the other day. I heard you talking to Kyra. Does Sean know that you were never really into him? Does he know that he was a target?" Insecurity was starting to give way to a sincere hurt and annoyance.

"But . . . what?" I asked, stunned. "It was just, you know, a—"

"Flirting is a game," he said. "But when real emotions get involved, you should stop playing around."

Was he talking about the two of us? What else could account for his irrational behavior? I was totally thrown; not ready to let him know how I felt, but having no idea how else to diffuse this situation. "It's not like that," I protested. "It was just practice. For—"

He shrugged. "Well, hopefully, talking to me was good practice too. Maybe all of our conversations will come in handy for you to refer back to one day, when it's the real deal. You know, with someone who isn't, um, like a *brother* to you."

"Gabe, that's not even—" *That's not even it,* I wanted to say. You're *the real deal! I was practicing for you!*

Brother? Gabe had obviously only heard bits of my conversation with Kyra, and somehow had managed to hear the part where she'd said he was like a brother to her.

Except, he had heard it wrong.

He thought he had heard it from me.

Suddenly, it all clicked in my mind. Kyra was right: He *did* like me. He had to. Otherwise why would he care if I saw him as a brother, cousin, or hell—even a grandfather? Why would he suddenly get so bent out of shape about "target practice"?

It was Kyra, I thought desperately. *You know her! How could you not have recognized her voice?*

But the words were stuck somewhere deep behind my rib cage. This was my moment, my chance to tell him how I felt. And it was all wrong. It was happening backward. He wasn't supposed to be angry. Surprised, maybe. Pleased, if there was a god in heaven watching over me. I'd even take amused. But not angry. Anything would be better than angry; maybe even no reaction at all. "You heard wrong," I said.

The look in his eyes indicated that he was more than finished with our conversation. "Whatever," he said, shrugging.

"*It was Kyra—*," I started again. My voice was a hoarse whisper, too low for him to catch even if he had been listening.

It didn't matter, though. He was already gone.

11/10, 2:34 p.m.
from: clnorton@woodmanuniv.edu
to: cbclarkson@woodmanuniv.edu
re: BALLS

I know, y'all are shocked at my language, but I've gotta be sassy now that I've finally grown me a pair!

Crazy how we've managed to completely

miss each other the last couple of days; whenever I'm home, it seems like you're sleeping. But I've got huge news: I talked to Anu! I think things are going to be cool, starting now. Can we meet at Brew and Gold at 5:15? I want to rehash.

11/10, 3:01 p.m.
from: cbclarkson@woodmanuniv.edu
to: clnorton@woodmanuniv.edu
re: You kiss your mother with that mouth?

Yes, I'm shocked and appalled. And dying to hear your story. Save a seat if you get there first, okay?

—xx

The last thing I wanted to do, really, was meet up with Charlie. Of course, I was thrilled that things seemed to be working out for her and her pledge sister; I knew how important the Tri-Delts were to her, and I wanted her to be happy. But I couldn't bear the embarrassment of breaking the news to her of my abject failure on the Gabe front.

It had been a full twenty-four hours

since our humiliating encounter (or, if you want to get technical about it, *my* humiliating encounter. I don't imagine that Gabe was at all humiliated by our little exchange). After Gabe had fled the lecture hall I had basically retreated to my bedroom and, under the covers, sought refuge in Chinese food and trashy magazines. At some point, I guess I fell asleep. It must have been hours before Charlie came home, because I don't actually remember hearing her come in. Today I had pulled myself together for classes, but that was about it. I'd avoided the dining halls, the library, the campus center . . . even the quad. I wasn't interested in running into anyone.

So it was with no small amount of trepidation that I wandered into Brew and Gold at five fifteen on the dot, cautiously scanning the room to find Charlie while remaining as invisible as I possibly could. She hadn't arrived yet, so I ordered my drink and collapsed into a sofa in the most remote corner of the room. Someone had abandoned the day's copy of the *Chronicle* on the side table next to me. I picked it up and began to casually flip through it, but pushed it aside again when I saw Gabe's byline. For once, I didn't want to read his piece.

"Sorry, sorry, sorry."

Suddenly Charlie was standing over me, unwrapping layer upon layer from her person. I laughed; it was mid-November, and the air had a definite snap to it, but only a Southerner would have overreacted like this. "Babe, what are you going to do when it snows?" I teased.

"That's when I get my mom to send along the electric blanket," she said, completely deadpan. "Anyway, I need a coffee. Save my seat!"

Five minutes later she was back on the couch, squished against the cushions and surrounded by her puffy outerwear. She looked warm, comfortable, and blissfully content.

"Details, please," I prompted.

"Well," she began, "I took your advice. I decided that I needed to nip this whole thing in the bud. I mean, my relationship with Anu can't be based on this messed-up dynamic or it will never improve—even after I'm initiated!"

"Agreed," I said. "In fact, I think as a general rule, you should always plan to follow my advice."

"I intend to!" she said. "See, I sent her an e-mail asking if she'd meet me at the café down in Davis Square. Yesterday. And she did."

"Was it awkward city?" I asked.

She nodded, taking a sip of her coffee. "At first. She walked in completely stiff. You could tell she wasn't eager to be there. But I was really frank—in a polite way. I told her that I felt we'd gotten off on the wrong foot, but that as a pledge it was really important to me to have a good relationship with my sisters, and especially my big sister, and that if there was something specific that I had done, I wished she would tell me so that I could fix the situation. And I think she was just so embarrassed—because, of course, I hadn't done anything, you know, and here I was trying to address the problem even though she'd made herself so unapproachable."

"So what did she say?"

"Well, at first she got a little bit defensive, pointing out a few things that I'd done wrong here and there."

"Bitch," I hissed.

"Well, yeah, but she was smart; she only stuck to facts. I mean, I've messed up now and then."

"Who hasn't?" I asked incredulously.

"That was exactly my point. And then I went, blow by blow, through each of the mistakes that had bothered her so much, and I talked about how I thought her treatment of me was different from the other big sisters' treatment of their little sisters, and even her treatment of other sisters. And I think I broke her down. She apologized. And she told me that maybe she'd been overreacting. Apparently Zach has been messing with her for ages now, and she can't even bring it up with him anymore because it always leads to a fight. And so she feels really frustrated and powerless, and that's why she was always taking it out on me."

"That's lame," I offered, somewhat less than helpfully.

"True," Charlie agreed. "But she's my big sister, and I have to get along with her, lame or not. So I'm just glad it's out in the open. And then she told me that she really respected the fact that I stood up to her."

"As I predicted!" I said, pantomiming patting myself on the back.

"Whatever, you're brilliant," Charlie said, laughing. "Thank you for forcing me to do this."

"Anytime," I said. I hugged her. "I'm so glad this worked out for you."

"Yeah! It's amazing how both of our situations worked out so nicely. What were the odds?" she said, beaming.

"Um, I guess not so good," I replied, biting my lip. "Because my situation? Yeah, not so much with the working out. Gabe's been avoiding me. He overheard me talking about 'target practice' with Kyra and flipped. He thinks that I think of him like a brother—total long story—and that he was just another 'target' to me. He won't even talk to me now."

"What?" Charlie stared at me, genuinely confused. "No way. I thought you guys had hashed it all out. At least, that's what I got from his personal."

Huh?

"Once more, with feeling, Charlie," I

said, commanding myself to take deep, even breaths. "What personal?"

She reached for the crumpled paper I'd recently discarded. "You didn't see? What's wrong with you? I thought checking the personals was the first thing you did every day."

I grabbed it from her and flipped to the back, skimming greedily.

There it was. The leftmost column, halfway down the page.

CB—ARTSY—EVEN ROTATORS SOMETIMES MAKE MISTAKES. PLEASE COME BACK AND PRACTICE ON ME. 4:45 ON THE QUAD IN FRONT OF BURNHAM.

I glanced at my watch. It was five thirty. "Shit." I looked at Charlie, desperate.

Her eyes were wide. "I just assumed you were coming from meeting him. I thought you'd have a cute anecdote to tell."

I looked down at my watch again, and then back to Charlie.

She put her hands on my shoulders. "Claudia. Go. Now."

I ran.

In my state of hysteria, Memorial Steps had become an Olympic-caliber obstacle course. As I climbed them two at a time I cursed myself for being so antigym. On the off chance that Gabe was still waiting on the quad, I'd be a crumpled, sweaty mess by the time I got to him.

Of course, odds were that he'd be gone.

The thought propelled me forward forcefully. It skittered across my brain with every bound: *Be there, be there, be there.*

I paused momentarily at the top of the steps to catch my breath. My eyes flickered across the grassy expanse. Of course, Burnham was due north of where I stood. Another sprint. I was just thankful I wasn't a smoker. I could see figures in front of the tall, brick building, but they were too far away to make out in detail. I sucked my breath in again and ran for it.

As I grew closer I could see the outlines of the figures more clearly. One was short, wearing baggy pants, colorful sneakers, and a baseball cap. Not Gabe. The other was a tall, redheaded woman. Also not Gabe. My pace slowed and I came to a staggering halt, leaning against one of the columns of the building. I slumped over, dejected. I had missed him.

"You all right?" the boy with the baseball cap asked me. From this proximity I could see he was Latino. *Definitely* not Gabe.

"I, uh . . . I was looking for someone. Have you seen a guy around here—tall, skinny, dark hair?"

The boy shrugged. "Nope. I've been here for a while, now. No one's come by."

Oh. So it wasn't that he'd come and gone, but rather that he'd stood me up.

Much better.

I would have just shoved off, back to the dorm, back to bed—or maybe even to find Gabe and demand to know what gave. But, as it was, my little impromptu workout had left me tired. I slid down to the ground and hunkered against the column, contemplating. I checked my watch for the umpteenth time. It read five forty-five. An hour later than Gabe's proposed meeting. Maybe my watch was slow, though. Or fast. Or something, *anything* that meant he hadn't blown me off completely. He'd never have written a personal like that if he didn't *want* to see me, after all.

Would he?

"What time do you have?" I asked cap-boy wearily.

"Five forty-five."

I froze. I knew that voice.

Slowly, I looked up. My gaze panned first across a scuffed pair of Adidas, and then over a worn pair of deep chocolate cords. Then the corners of a flannel shirt, and over that, a nubby wool sweater.

Topped off, of course, with my favorite blue-green eyes. Which were, finally, looking straight into my own. And twinkling. "I'm such a loser. I'm so sorry I'm late."

He reached out a hand and helped me to my feet. Now we were standing face-to-face. "Why *were* you late?" I asked. I tried to sound stern, but the smile that stretched across my cheeks was giving me away.

"I had to get some stuff together for you." He dug into his messenger bag. "First this."

I looked at it. It was a CD. He'd made a colorful, graffiti-style label for it: MAD SALAD, LIVE AT THE TIN ROOM.

My smile threatened to slide right off my face and wrap itself around him.

"Oh!" I said, realizing. "I'm going to have to delete some stuff off of my iPod. It's full. Don't worry," I joked. "The Backstreet Boys can go. You're amazing." I pulled back from him suddenly, self-conscious. "*Why* are you so amazing now?"

He shrugged. "I talked to my 'sister.'" At my confusion, he clarified. "Kyra. She explained everything. Like, especially how I was being a moron."

It's possible that Kyra has her good points, then.

He handed me a deck of cards. And another box, this one wrapped in newspaper, which I hastily ripped off. "A Nerf dartboard?" I asked, puzzled.

"For 'target practice,' Claud."

I shoved him. "You're ridiculous," I said. But I was laughing.

"I *am* ridiculous. I was ridiculous the other day. I totally overreacted. I'm sorry."

"Apology accepted."

"Anyway," he continued, "it's supposed to snow tomorrow. I was thinking you could come by my place and we could set the dartboard up, stay in, and play games all weekend."

It sounded perfect, except for one thing.

"I'm done playing games, Gabe," I said softly, reaching up and running my fingers across his face.

He circled one arm around me and buried the other deep in my hair. "Does that mean you finished? Thirty guys?"

I paused for a moment, contemplating. Then I remembered: baseball-cap boy. "As a matter of fact, yes. Just before you got here," I said.

"Perfect timing," he said, eyes gleaming with emotion.

I offered him a small, self-satisfied grin. "And here I was going to ask what took you so long."

Gabe's response was to lean forward and kiss me, deep and full on the lips. I closed my eyes, breathing in his scent, running my fingers through his hair, down his neck, across his back, taking in all of him against me. I'd always imagined that kissing Gabe would be electric; I'd had no idea that I'd feel it in my fingertips, toes, the pit of my stomach. . . . I could barely stand.

I guess he had the same reaction, because we pulled apart simultaneously, each of us struggling to catch our breath and our balance once again. "Wow," Gabe said, reaching out to brush my hair from my eyes.

I grinned and grabbed at the front of his sweater, pulling him back to me and kissing him softly again. I traced my way up the side of his face gently, until I'd reached his ear. I stood on tiptoe and whispered to him just one word:

"Bull's-eye."

Epilogue

11/16, 7:52 p.m.
from: cbclarkson@woodmanuniv.edu
to: kissandtellen@shemail.net,
clnorton@woodmanuniv.edu
re: All's well that ends well

Hi there, ladies:

Just back from my pop culture midterm. Thank god Gabe and I made up in time to study together, because favorite class or no, it wasn't easy. But it's definite: I'm going to be a media studies major! I just can't resist the thought of watching movies for credit. Bio, child psych, and women's history are fine, and believe it or not, I think I'm pulling a B– in comp sci.

Ellen: Charlie was initiated last night. She came home wearing a balloon animal crown and a mustache that, near as we can tell, was drawn on in Sharpie. So we're still working on removing that. But she's thrilled enough that I don't think she even minds looking like Groucho Marx for a few more days.

Meanwhile she has settled in enough with Troy that she has finally stopped dragging me to the gym with her. Either they go together, or she skips it entirely. I'm very impressed. She even mentioned possibly paying him a visit over Thanksgiving break 'cause they live kind of nearby. Staggering, what love will do to you.

Thanksgiving. Is it really next week? Gabe's going back to Highland Park, of course, which is a little bit too far for me to just "stop by." And even though he invited me, I told him I wasn't sure I felt comfortable spending the holiday weekend with his family. Which, of course, he understood. Kyra promised me she'd save me a piece of pie, which I think was her way of reminding me that she'll always have history with him. But I don't care. After all, she was the one who ultimately brought us together.

Okay, maybe I care a little bit. I'm only human, after all. BUT SO IS SHE, it turns out!!!

What with the freak snowstorm that hit this week, we've all basically been snowed in. Thank god for the games Gabe brought. I've been practicing on the Nerf dartboard every day. I'm an ace now, no joke. Bull's-eye every time. Gabe says it's a shame I'm retired from "target practice" 'cause I'm a real ringer. He says my talents are wasted.

But I say I've already won first prize.

—xx

About the Author

Micol Ostow is an editor and writer of books for children, tweens, and teens. She lives and works in New York City. When she's not writing, she enjoys running, reading, eating chocolate, and watching bad television (in no particular order and sometimes even all at once). She has never played "target practice." But she thinks it would be fun. Contact Micol at: micolz@aol.com.

LOL at this sneak peek of

My Summer as a Giant Beaver
By Jamie Ponti

A new Romantic Comedy from Simon Pulse

This is so not right.

It's the first day of summer vacation and I'm already up at six thirty in the morning. Officially, I've sworn off overpriced coffee until I've paid for the car. But this is an emergency, so I break my Starbucks rule and get a venti cappuccino.

By the time I reach Magic Waters, the caffeine has done its trick and I'm nearly coherent. I need to find my supervisor before orientation starts so I can beg for a different job. (Mermaid show or no mermaid show, I still owe my parents $1,250.)

She's cool about it when I explain my problem and she even arranges for me to stay in the entertainment department. This is great because entertainment pays almost a dollar an hour more than any other department. The job, though, is with the zoo crew. This is not great.

The zoo crew is what they call the costumed characters who roam around the park and dance in the parade. A job like that might be cool at a place like Disney World, where the costumes are well made and the characters are beloved. But at Magic Waters, it's like a completely lame school play.

I get assigned to play Eager Beaver.

I'm not joking. That's really his name. Or her name. No one really knows if Eager Beaver is a boy or a girl. They only know that Eager Beaver likes to dance around the Rapid River Log Flume—"The Rootin' Tootinest ride in the Wild Wild West."

Next, I go to the wardrobe warehouse, which could not be freakier. When I open the door, I run smack into the disembodied head of Ollie Otter. All the character heads are stored on posts right by the front door. When you're not expecting it, it looks like you've stumbled into some bizarro cartoon headhunter ceremony.

I report to the costume counter, which is manned by a woman who I swear is the actual Mrs. Claus. She's got rosy red cheeks, granny glasses, and a sewing apron.

"Good morning," she says in a manner way too jolly for this time of day. "Who are you?"

"Jane," I answer. "Jane Quincy."

She gives a disapproving look and points her finger at me in a way that makes me want to snap it off.

"You may be Jane Quincy out there." She motions to the door. "But once you pass through these portals you become one of our magical characters."

I think this is going to take more than just one venti.

"So let's try again. Who are you?"

"Eager Beaver," I mumble, still trying to rub the sleep out of my eyes, hoping this is all a dream.

"Well you don't sound so eager to me," she says with a laugh. "But we can work on that."

She disappears into a back room and returns with my costume. It's hideous. She hands me a fur bodysuit that weighs a ton, a pair of four-fingered gloves, and huge black boots that will completely ruin my feet. Then she goes over to the giant rack o' heads (God, that freaks me out) and pulls off Eager Beaver's noggin. I don't know why he's so happy, but he's got the biggest bucktoothed smile you ever saw.

I seriously consider running out the door.

Mrs. Claus misreads my state of shock as a case of magical wonder and awe.

She smiles warmly. "Don't worry, dear. You're perfect for Eager Beaver." She says this as though it's a good thing.

"Why is that?" I want to know. But I'm more than a little scared of what the answer might be.

"Because you're so flat-chested," she replies. "The costume won't bind in the bust."

At this point, I want to kill Mrs. Claus. But I'm pretty sure that will cost me my job and ultimately my car. So instead, I just smile. "Lucky me."

"Why don't you go try it on," she adds.

The costume, me, and my flat chest all head into the locker room, which reeks of a strange brew of polyester, sweat, and fiberglass. Despite the assurances of Mrs. Claus, the costume could not be more uncomfortable.

The fur body (think bad shag carpet) is about eight million degrees. Right from the start it makes my skin itch. The fiberglass head has only two teensy eye slits, which make it impossible to see. The head also weighs so much that if I lean just a little too much one way or another, I lose my balance.

The worst part, though, is the tail. Eager Beaver has a gigantic tail. It's even gigantic by cartoon standards. It pulls down on my butt so much, I feel like my pants are falling down.

I spend the next few minutes walking around the locker room trying to develop my "beaver legs." In short order, I trip over my tail, knock down a potted plant, trip over my tail again, smack into a Coke machine, and slam headfirst into the wall of lockers. (Altogether, not unlike the night Becca and I mixed rum and Diet Coke under the mistaken belief that they were to be blended in equal portions.)

Orientation turns out to be a lot like the first day of school. By the time I figure out where the bathroom is, everyone else has already broken up into little groups. It doesn't take long to see that there's a pecking order at

Magic Waters, just like there is at Ruby Beach High. The mermaids sit alone at the top of the food chain.

They're the stars. (They even wear matching baby blue warm-ups with their names stitched just above their oh-so-perfect left breasts.) The Zoo Crew is somewhere in the middle, just above food service and the janitorial staff.

After an initial welcome speech, everyone goes off into smaller groups with their departments.

While Crystal and the mer-chicks pose for their lobby photos, I learn the beaver dance from a"choreographer" whose name is pronounced "Chris" but spelled "Krys." The dance is pretty much just me hopping around and shaking my tail. Krys, of course, is not satisfied.

"You're a beaver, not a bunny," he says, clapping his hands to the beat.

I have no idea what he means, but I act like I do and just keep hopping and shaking. Luckily I am rescued by Platypus Rex, who informs Krys that Ollie Otter is having big trouble mastering the parade march.

When Kris rushes over to help Ollie,

Rex hustles me out a side door to a patio.

"You looked like you needed a break," he says as he takes off his platypus head and plops down on a bench.

"Thank you," I tell him as I ditch my giant beaver head. "My name's Jane."

"Grayson." We sort of shake hands, which is no easy task in our bulky costumes.

I try to get a good image of him, but it's hard. His hair is all stuffed into a bandana and his face is flushed from wearing the costume. I can only imagine how bad I look right now.

It turns out that Grayson's a senior at Fletcher—our rival high school. He's in his third summer as Platypus Rex. Unlike Krys and Mrs. Claus, he doesn't seem to take it so seriously.

He tells me the various zoo crew rules, which are plentiful. Characters are not allowed to talk (because it breaks the magic) and you can only sign autographs after special training to make sure you do it right. (I'm not kidding.)

You're never allowed to take off your head when you're in a guest area because it really freaks kids out. (After my first encounter with the rack o' heads, I can relate.)

He also warns me that every single kid who comes into the park will feel the need to pull my tail. Despite my natural instinct, it is not all right for me to slug them when they do this.

We chat some more until Krys finds us and orders us back inside for more practice. Two hours later I stumble back into the locker room and collapse on the bench. I am totally exhausted. My face and hair are so covered in sweat that I don't even know where to begin.

As if on cue, Crystal and the other mermaids come in from their photo shoot. They don't mock or pick or even notice my existence. They don't have to.

They just smile their perfect smiles, toss their perfect hair, and heave their perfect (and fake) breasts. I was supposed to be one of them. I was supposed to be in a bikini, working on my tan and flirting with boys. Instead, I'm a giant beaver in a fur suit getting my tail yanked by bratty kids.

I watch them sashay by and realize a horrifying truth. The conspiracy to ruin my life is now complete.